Brute Strength ...

Diamondback reached around with both hands and grabbed fistfulls of greasy black hair at the back of Redwood's neck. He pulled with every bit of strength he had left, ignoring his own pain. Slowly he forced Redwood's head further and further backward. But still the giant wouldn't loosen his iron grip on Cord's spine. The muscles in Redwood's neck stood out like thick miners' rope as he strained against Cord's pull.

When he had finally forced Redwood's head back until the chin tilted toward the roof, Diamondback released one of his hands and jammed his forearm straight down into Redwood's exposed throat.

There was a horrible croaking as Redwood's arms sprang free, dropping Cord to his feet. Redwood's eyes were huge and bulging as he stumbled backwards, struggling to suck in air.

Cord leaped forward, his fists snapping into Redwood's face and body with unending regularity. He battered Redwood relentlessly until his own fists were numb.

Exhausted, Cord loaded everything into a left hook/right cross combination, whipping Redwood Sam's head back and forth like a Pennsylvania Dutch weather vane. Redwood's eyes rolled up into his head as he finally toppled over.

DIAMONDBACK

PIKE BISHOP

PINNACLE BOOKS   NEW YORK

To Leif Regvall, the fastest shooting, hardest loving, toughest MBA in the West.

DIAMONDBACK

Copyright © 1983 by Raymond Obstfeld

An original Pinnacle Books edition, published for the first time anywhere.

First printing, April, 1983

ISBN: 0-523-41948-1

Cover illustration by Aleta Jenks

Printed in the United States of America

PINNACLE BOOKS, INC.
1430 Broadway
New York, New York 10018

DIAMONDBACK

1.

"Don't get yourself killed," old Mathew O'Neill warned, his old worried face seamed with wrinkles like a decomposing pumpkin. He waved an ancient finger in Cord Diamondback's smooth impassive face. "Nor crippled either. Getting old is enough of a chore with all your parts working."

"Aw, Cord will murder him," young Jimmy Simms giggled excitedly, dropping the bucket of his mother's lard at Cord's bare feet. "I just know you will, Cord. Stone cold dead."

Cord Diamondback smiled but said nothing. He never liked to talk before a fight, not even to friends. Instead he concentrated on whipping his energy to a white hot intensity until it burned deep within his chest. He thought of it as if he were stoking a powerful locomotive, harnessing enough compressed steam to shove forty tons of chugging iron down a track. When it was time for talking, Cord could wield fancy words with the best of them. But when it was time for action, he considered talking as just a valve that allowed precious steam to escape. And right now he needed all that steam for this fight.

"Let me do that for you, Cord," Mathew offered, already scooping his boney hands into the mushy lard. He began vigorously rubbing the lard deep into

Cord's hands, especially the flat scarred knuckles. "You'd best slop some on your face," he cautioned. "That feller's got fists as big as ham hocks. Looks like he knows how to use them, too."

Cord nodded agreement. Earlier that day he'd caught a glimpse of his 250-pound opponent behind the saloon as he'd been crushing old packing crates with his bare hands just to warm up. This wasn't going to be an easy one.

"Want me to help you off with your shirt, Cord?" Jimmy asked, anxious to please. He reached over to unfasten the buttons.

"No!" Cord snapped, grabbing the boy's wrist.

Old Mathew looked up startled, spit out a squirt of tobacco juice between his stained teeth, and returned to massaging in the lard. His eyebrows knotted with concern.

Jimmy sagged, hurt and disappointed, his thirteen-year-old eyes misting slightly as he rubbed his wrist where Cord had held him.

Cord was immediately sorry, but it couldn't be helped. His life depended on that protective reflex. He knew that if anyone saw him without his shirt they'd instantly realize that Cord Diamondback wasn't his real name. Even in a jerkwater little town like this, people would recognize his true name—and remember what savage crime he was accused of. And if Jimmy or Mathew or any of the townsfolk hollering outside that door suspected who he really was, he'd have a rope cinched around his neck with no time for explanations for what he'd done that night or why.

That night. Five years ago. Cord remembered it as he always did, with a cold stab in his heart for his own terrible loss—and a hot ache of vengeance gnawing through his stomach like a starving rat. When that night was finally over his name had become known to every lawman and bounty hunter west of Missouri. Known and hated.

Well, he'd had his own reasons for what he'd done. And they were good enough for him.

"I want you to be real careful, Cord," Mathew said with a worried sigh as he wiped the excess lard on the seat of his dirty pants. "Little while ago I heard that feller spouting off how he was gonna split your face from forehead to chin. Real mean talk it was."

Cord winked at Jimmy, coaxing him out of his sulk.

Jimmy brightened immediately. "Yeah, Cord. And yesterday I seen him do just that to Mr. Cutter."

"Josiah Cutter?" Mathew asked.

"Yup. They was over in the Golden Springs Saloon having themselves a drinking contest. First, one would drink a shot of whiskey, then follow it with a mug of beer. Then the other would drink *two* shots of whiskey and follow them with another mug of beer. Then the other . . ."

"Yeah, yeah, Jimmy," Mathew said, his craggy face crumpled into impatient wrinkles, "I know what a drinking contest is. Just tell me what happened to Josiah Cutter."

"Well," Jimmy drawled, pleased to have both men's attention, "they'd been drinking for quite a while— more shots of whiskey than I could count anymore— and it looked like Mr. Cutter was going to win. Then suddenly that big ox waiting outside here swings around with his mug of beer still in his hands and clobbers poor Mr. Cutter right in the face with it." Jimmy smacked his little fist into his open palm. "Just like that. Ole Mr. Cutter sorta wobbles for a minute with the beer and blood gushing all over his face and everybody else afraid to help him. Then his eyes roll up into his head like this." He rolled up his eyes. ". . . and he flops face down on the ground. Couple of his teeth hit the floor before he did."

Mathew gave Cord a nervous look. Cord's face remained impassive, almost bored.

"And his face," Jimmy frowned, "it looked like somebody'd took to it with a straight razor. Doc Evens said he'd be wearing those scars for the rest of his life."

"Not to mention no teeth," Mathew grumbled, shaking his head. "That's one bad man out there, Cord."

Cord Diamondback reached over into the lard bucket, holding his breath as not to get sick from the rich greasy smell. He slapped the globs of warm lard around his high cheekbones, across his long square jaw, along his narrow crooked nose. Anywhere hard sharp knuckles might split skin.

Depending on how the light hit it, Cord's face shifted between cruelly handsome and just plain rugged. It was a composite of conflicting angles intersecting on a thin confident mouth. A mouth that could smile easily or frown with withering severity. It was a chaotic face, given order only by a pair of dark dominating eyes. Dangerous eyes that were dark beyond color, as if they had too many colors crowding in all at once. But it was the skin that fascinated women the most. Despite his years at sea and riding under a punishing sun, his skin remained strangely pale and smooth. Which made it difficult to judge his age. This disturbed those who assumed he was at least part Indian because of his unusual name. The truth would have disturbed them even more.

Mathew handed Cord an almost-clean bandanna to

blot up the excess lard. It wouldn't do to have sweat mixed with lard dripping into his eyes during the fight.

"Come on out, ya skinny son of a railyard bitch," the big man called from the other side of the closed door, then laughed like a rusty gate hinge.

From inside the tiny room, Diamondback could hear the crowd laughing too. Nearly the whole town must have been out there. Including the town's lawmen. He just hoped his new clean-shaven appearance was different enough from the last wanted posters he'd seen.

"Let's go!" someone in the crowd shouted impatiently. "I still got me an acre to plow 'fore supper."

Some in the crowd were shouting approval of the man's demands. Others were making chicken clucking noises.

"*Shut up!*" Jimmy hollered, his little fists threatening the door that separated them from the taunting crowd. "Just shut up!"

Jimmy swung his red face around to look at Cord, who merely winked and smiled again. But that was enough for Jimmy, who burst out into his own huge grin.

Cord didn't blame the people outside. They didn't know him enough to like or dislike him. They didn't know that under his real name he was wanted for what newspapers had called "the worst crime of the decade." Nor did they even recognize his adopted name, the one he'd been living under for the past few years, though it also carried a strong reputation. But of a completely different kind. All these people knew for certain was that he'd ridden into Walkers Rest less than three weeks ago and had kept pretty much to himself, except when sweeping and mending stables at Mathew O'Neill's livery barn. And that the only friends he'd made in town were Mathew O'Neill himself, who at the age of sixty-four ought to know better than to take up with rough-looking strangers; the widow Amy Simms, whose husband's long string of bad luck ended last year when, as a teller at Walkers Rest Bank, he was shot by a stray bullet from a retired sheriff during a holdup; and her skinny tow-headed son, Jimmy.

The big man outside was a stranger here too, but most townsfolk had at least heard about him. And those that could read had read about him. His name was Redwood Sam Taggert, and he'd once fought heavyweight champion Paddy Ryan to a 47-round draw in Mississippi City. Some had also heard that Redwood Sam had killed a man in the twenty-third round last year over at the Billows County Fair, but others defended him by saying the man wasn't dead, just paralyzed from the waist down. Now Redwood Sam travelled around the country taking on local toughs for from $100 to $500 a bout and whatever sidebets his manager could arrange.

Most of the people in Walkers Rest were surprised that a drifter like this Diamondback fellow, especially one with a name that sounded awfully Indian, could come up with that kind of cash. Rumors were snaking around town that he was a barnburner who'd torched the last place he'd worked, killing his employer and stealing the money. But these rumors were started by Redwood Sam's manager, so nobody really believed it, though everybody did their part in passing it along.

Actually, Cord had only $322 in cash with Mathew O'Neill putting up $100, and Jimmy's mother, who

Cord had gotten to know on a very personal level, putting up the difference.

"Let's go!" Redwood Sam demanded again. This time there was no humor in the booming voice, no laughter. Just business.

Cord Diamondback slowly stood up, stretched, rolled his head around a few times, first to the left, then to the right. Bones popped into place.

Mathew O'Neill also stood up, still wiping the greasy lard from his hands onto his pants. "Good luck, Cord. Not that I think you'll be needing it."

"Heck," Jimmy piped in, "they'll be scraping that big guy's guts off the walls by the time old Cord's done with him."

"'*Old* Cord,' huh?" Diamondback repeated and laughed for the first time that day, his handsome head thrown back, his dark eyes almost closed. He clapped Mathew on the back and patted Jimmy on the head, ruffling big long blonde hair. Then he stepped out of Mathew's tiny business office, ducking through the narrow door, and into the main barn of the stable.

The sudden explosion of cheering bounced along the wooden rafters, peppering the crowd below with loosened dust. Cord moved forward ignoring the cheers. Very few, if any, were for him.

He trotted over to the milking stool and bucket of warm water that represented his corner, pushing the sleeves of his skin-tight longjohns up past his elbows. There were a few appreciative murmurs at the sight of his powerfully sculpted physique, apparent even through the shirt. His tight muscles were already shimmering with sweat.

"Take if off," one of Kate Laney's girls from the

nearby cathouse taunted with a lewd whistle. "I came here to see some beefcake."

Most of the crowd laughed, though some of the marrieds pretended they didn't see, hear, or know her in any way.

Cord glanced across the barn at Redwood Sam Taggert, already stripped to the waist and grinning menacingly through huge yellow horse teeth. He was an awesome mass of muscle and cruelty, an effect heightened by the dark tattoo of a heavy chain wrapped twice around his thick neck.

Cord bent over and grabbed his ankles, loosening the muscles in his back. Right now he had to empty his head of anything that might interfere with what was about to happen. He had to forget why he couldn't take off his shirt, why he had to use this made-up name, why he had to be careful about changing his appearance so often. It was like draining a creek bed until all that was left was the dry smooth stones and mud baking in the sun. That's what was inside him now.

Dry stones.

Yet, despite everything, he was strangely exhilarated, the way he always was before a fight. It wasn't nervousness exactly, though when he looked at hulking Redwood Sam Taggert and his bizarre tattoo he thought it should be. No, it was something more fulfilling, almost adventurous, as if he were about to purge himself of some great burden. The way he used to feel when he was eighteen and standing in the rocking bow of a New Bedford whaler, his sharpened harpoon poised at his chest, his eager face dripping with salty Atlantic spray. He remembered his hard young muscles tensed and anxious, just waiting for a grey sperm whale as big as this barn to break surface. In those days he'd always felt a little sorry for any whale unlucky enough to come within striking distance of his hungry harpoon. But that feeling had been burned out of him one night in a San Francisco mansion, in a baptism of spurting blood and ungodly screams. The only difference now, Cord thought as he smiled over at scowling Redwood Sam, was that he didn't feel sorry anymore. He didn't feel anything.

"You Cord Diamondback?" someone behind him demanded.

Cord turned slowly around. A young woman not more than twenty-two years old was standing between Mathew and Jimmy. She was wearing a man's riding outfit, still dusty and sweat-stained from a hard ride, but there was no hiding her sex or steel-edged beauty. Still, she tried. Strapped to her narrow waist was a Colt Peacemaker .45, rigged onto a quick-fire bolt rather than a holster, allowing the gun to be fired by swiveling it from the hip. It was more fancy than effective, and Cord hadn't seen too many of them lately. And never one strapped to a woman. She was trying awfully hard to look mean and tough as she studied Cord up and down with a mixture of surprise and disappointment.

"Sorry, Cord," Mathew shrugged. "Lady wanted to know where Cord Diamondback was. Said it was important."

"That's okay, Matt." Cord faced the young woman, his dark eyes nailed to her pale blue ones. "Whatever it is will have to wait, lady. I'm a bit busy right now."

"You about ready, Diamondback?" Deputy Marshal Fenton asked from the middle of the cleared area that was to be the fight ring. Deputy Marshal Fenton was the referee. He also had a $25 bet with Ed Hemmings, the barkeeper at the Golden Springs, in favor of Redwood Sam.

"Yeah," Cord nodded. "I'm ready."

Deputy Marshall Fenton moved his cigar, a gift from Redwood Sam's manager, from one side of his mouth to the other using only his lips. "You ready, Redwood?"

The big man across the barn cracked his knuckles and sneered. "Let's get started."

"Mr. Diamondback," the young woman said urgently, as Cord turned away from her. "I've been riding most of four days now to see you."

"What about?"

"Well," she looked at Mathew and Jimmy, uncertain whether to speak in their presence. Not having any choice, she continued in a hoarse whisper. "I want to hire you."

"To do what?"

She rested her hand on her pistol. "Some judging. That's what you do, isn't it?"

"Sometimes," he said calmly, but there was an obvious difference in him now. His eyes shone darkly as no one in this town had ever seen them shine before, like a glowing branding iron sizzling against a block of ice. "We'll talk after the fight."

"Don't you want the details?"

"After the fight." He motioned with his head for her to step back. She hesitated, then followed his advice. Everyone else moved back a step too. Everyone except big Redwood Sam. He moved forward.

So did Cord Diamondback.

2.

Deputy Marshal Fenton dragged the heel of his boot in a straight line down the center of the cleared area. About a yard away he dug another parallel line.

"Now, you boys know the rules a sight better than me, but it won't do no harm to go over 'em once more. A lot of folks around here ain't never seen a real prizefight before." He paused a moment to acknowledge the nods of assent from the crowd. "Now, we'll be using the, uh, the, um . . ."

"London Prize Ring rules of 1853," Cord offered. He hadn't expected they'd use the tamer Marquis of Queensberry rules, even though the London Prize Ring rules had been outlawed by this and nearly every other state in the country. Most people still considered the new rules with its padded gloves and three-minute rounds to be unmanly. Not enough blood. Not enough pain. It didn't matter to Cord one way or the other. He didn't mind blood or pain.

"Yeah, them's the rules I mean," Deputy Marshal Fenton said, shifting his unlit cigar to the other side of his mouth again. "That means a round lasts until somebody is knocked down. After that you've got thirty seconds rest."

"Hell, Marshal," Kate Laney hollered, "I give my girls more rest than that between rounds."

11

Everyone roared with laughter, including Deputy Marshal Fenton. "And your girls probably take more of a pounding too, Kate." He turned back to the fighters. "Now, at the end of that thirty seconds, you'll have eight more seconds to come to the center of the ring and toe your lines. And don't worry none about messing up my lines during the fight, I'll be happy to make new ones." He chuckled and the crowd joined in with approving laughter. He waved happily at them and continued. "If one of you don't come out to your line, you'll be declared 'not up to scratch' and lose the fight. Any questions, boys?"

"Let's get on with it, Sheriff," Redwood Sam growled.

"Deputy Marshal," Fenton corrected good-naturedly. "Okay, boys, toe your mark."

The two men placed their toes on the lines Deputy Marshal Fenton had made. Redwood Sam glared down at Cord from a height of about six-and-a-half feet, a six-inch advantage. He was making bull-like snorts that Cord knew were more for the audience's sake than anything else.

Deputy Marshal Fenton held up his right hand between the two men, looked first at Redwood Sam, then at Cord Diamondback. Then he dropped his hand. "Go fight!" he shouted to a round of excited applause, and hurried backwards to get out of the way.

Redwood Sam immediately charged forward, his huge tree-trunk legs kicking up dust with each movement. His thick muscular arms were far apart, as if he were more intent on tackling Cord than boxing him. And since wrestling was permitted under these rules, Cord figured that's exactly what he was planning to do.

Cord shuffled backwards, bouncing on his toes, shifting his movement to the left, then to the right. He didn't want Redwood Sam to get within bear-hug reach; if he did, Redwood would fall on him and there would be no way Cord could win this fight. He'd be lucky to be able to walk away after it was all over.

"Come here you little cock-a-doodle-doo." Redwood Sam smiled through huge yellow horse teeth and waved for Cord to come closer. "Redwood Sam won't hurt you. Permanently." Several men in the crowd hooted their approval, and several others began clucking again.

Cord didn't care. He moved at his own steady pace, aware that this was a fight that couldn't afford to go the usual twenty or thirty or even forty rounds. After that long in the ring with this giant, even if he won there wouldn't be enough left of him to heal. And he had to be in good enough shape to take the job he'd just been offered. That was the most important thing right now. It had nothing to do with the woman's obvious beauty. Her fiery good looks and pert figure weren't enough to make him take the job. Nor was it just the money. It was never just the money when it came to that kind of work. It was the nature of the job that intrigued him. "Judging" as she'd called it.

Redwood Sam lumbered forward again, then swung a looping left hook at Diamondback's head. Cord ducked it easily, gliding off to the left. Redwood looked puzzled at first, then angry.

"Whatch ya afraid of, boy?"

Cord said nothing, just kept gliding around him in a big circle.

"Stand still, damn it," Redwood hollered and lunged

at Cord with both hands spread into giant claws. One clamped down on Cord's shoulder and began to squeeze. Cord felt the bones begin to shift painfully under the crunching grip. He quickly twisted his body, spinning away from Redwood Sam. Without hesitating, he slid under the groping outstretched arms and fired off two powerful punches into the giant's kidney. Redwood sank to his knees with a startled gasp.

"End of round one," Deputy Marshal Fenton declared, his open hands waving over his head. "Get to your corners."

There was some light booing as Redwood stumbled back to his corner, rubbing the red splotch over his kidney.

Diamondback sat quietly on his stool and waited.

"Water, Cord?" Mathew asked, lifting the ladle full of warm water from the bucket. He plucked out a sprig of straw.

"Not yet, Matt. But just make sure nobody spits tobacco or pours anything in it."

Mathew nodded.

"Would they do that?" Jimmy asked with some shock.

"I've seen it happen before."

"Time!" Deputy Marshal Fenton said. "Toe your mark." He'd scratched two fresh boot lines in the middle of the ring.

"Come on, Redwood," somebody in the crowd yelled. "Quit dancing with him."

"Yeah," someone else cackled. "You boys ain't engaged, are you?"

Redwood Sam's large watermelon head snapped around, searching the crowd with tiny pig eyes for the men who'd said those things. Cord had the feeling that fight or no fight, if he'd have found them he'd have taken off through the crowd after them like a wild boar. When Redwood finally gave up looking through the crowd, he leveled his angry glare of Cord.

But there was something new in his expression now, a crazy vacant glint, the kind Cord had seen before in the eyes of men who'd made up their minds to kill. A glint Cord had seen too often in his own eyes.

"Fight!" Deputy Marshal Fenton said and the two men moved toward each other.

Redwood didn't lunge this time. He used his body wisely, cutting the ring down to size, forcing Cord to move in smaller and smaller arcs until he was trapped in a corner formed by the pressing crowd. Even as it was happening, Cord understood what Redwood was doing, but he was unable to prevent it. Now, with nowhere left to go, he waited for the inevitable.

And it came.

All 250 pounds of it, swinging wildly, hoping to land one mighty death blow. Arms thrashed like pickaxes, most glancing harmlessly off Cord's shoulders and arms. But occasionally one would dig into a kidney or dent a rib.

Cord had to attack. He lashed out with a short left jab, smashing Redwood squarely in the nose. The nose made a funny cracking sound as it flattened against Redwood's face. Blood spurted out of both nostrils, spraying Redwood's massive chest. But the giant didn't seem to even notice. He just kept wading forward, his fists flying. Cord managed to continue blocking most of the punches. But there were too many, each more powerful than the last.

Finally a solid uppercut crunched into Cord's mouth

and he felt his teeth bite through his lower lip. Then the lip went numb. His eyes began to water until he was having trouble seeing and the taste of warm sour blood curdled his stomach.

Instantly something hard and sharp, an elbow probably, chopped down on his shoulder. The shoulder went numb too. His legs began to buckle. He concentrated on keeping his legs moving, but now they seemed fat and clumsy, as if caught in a deep swamp. He could barely hear the crowd's excited howling.

"And here's another one," Redwood Sam hissed, swinging his elbow into Cord's neck.

Diamondback felt a jolt of lightning climb his spine and sizzle its way into his brain. He crumbled to the ground. While hunched there, he lifted his dazed head in time to see Redwood's rock-hard knee explode against his cheek. The cheekbone popped loudly in his ears and he knew it was broken. A few drops of blood began to seep out of his left ear.

"That's round two," Deputy Marshal Fenton said, rushing forward. "Get to your corners now."

Jimmy and Mathew hurriedly dragged Cord back to his corner, balancing him on the milking stool and splashing a ladle full of water in his face. Mathew mopped the blood as gently as he could, but Cord still winced at his touch.

"I could use that drink of water now," Cord grimaced.

Jimmy quickly scooped up another ladle of water and handed it to Cord.

Mathew poured some water over his bloody bandanna and continued dabbing Diamondback's face. "Look's bad, Cord. That cheek is broke for sure. And your lip looks about twice the size it ought to be." Mathew stared into Cord's eyes. "If I didn't know better, I'd say that boy's planning to make sure you never fight him or anyone else again."

"Aw, you'll get him this time, Cord," Jimmy said. But his face was troubled.

"Quiet, Jimmy," Mathew scolded. "Cord, don't you figure your life is worth more than five hundred dollars?"

"Time!" Deputy Marshal Fenton said.

Diamondback slowly pulled himself to his feet. "Matt, I figure five hundred dollars is exactly what my life is worth. That may even be a little generous."

"Okay, Cord, I guess you know what you're doing."

Cord grinned through thick swollen lips. "Don't I look it?"

When the two men stepped up to their respective lines, Redwood growled. "I have a feeling about this round, tough guy. A feeling that you ain't going to like it much."

"Fight!" Deputy Marshal Fenton said, and backed away into the safety of the crowd.

Redwood Sam jumped forward, cocky after his success in the last round. But Cord was back on his toes, moving in a wide circle, though not with as much bounce or speed as before.

Redwood grinned and began his stalking movements again, cutting the ring into sections, not allowing Cord to move around him. When he had Cord cornered again, he charged in swinging, his fists thumping down like flaming meteors.

The first punch glanced off the side of Cord's head, but it was solid enough to stagger him backwards a few feet into the crowd. A couple of men, farmers from the smell of them, kept Cord from falling. But they all backed up hurriedly when they saw Redwood stampeding towards them, eyes insanely wide and mouth grunting like a grizzly.

Cord tucked his head down and raised his arms, took a few heavy blows on the shoulders and forearms, then spun off to the side and buried his fist wrist-deep into Redwood's stomach. Redwood groaned loudly and clamped his hands over his aching stomach. Instantly, Cord threw three quick jabs into his face, following with a powerful right cross that carried all of his granite-hard 178 pounds behind it.

Redwood's head snapped around, spraying some of his blood on the nearby crowd. The giant's nose seemed to be barely hanging onto his face and his lip was torn all the way up to his cheek. Still, he wouldn't go down.

Diamondback slipped in closer to work on the kidneys, but he had underestimated Redwood's strength. Once within range, the man-mountain wrapped a huge hairy arm around Cord's waist and jerked him forward off his feet. With his hands at the base of Cord's spine, Redwood used his oppressive weight to bend Cord backward at the waist. The bones in Cord's back crackled like a campfire.

Cord grit his teeth against the pain and began clubbing Redwood on the side of the head as if he were a runaway stallion. But Redwood just smiled through blood-soaked teeth, tightening his bone-crunching grip. The tattooed chain circling his neck expanded as the muscles in his neck flexed.

"Ain't you gonna stop this, Fenton?" Mathew demanded of the lawman.

"Can't, Mathew. The round ain't over till one of them falls to the ground or just gives up."

"But Cord's being held so's he can't fall."

"Well," Deputy Marshal Fenton said, shifting his cigar, "he can still give up, can't he?"

"Not likely," Mathew frowned. "Not him."

Cord grunted as he felt the scraping of bones in his lower back. Through the agonizing pain, he imagined them grinding each other to a fine chalky dust. It was more pain than he could ever remember but he struggled to remain conscious. Somewhere deep inside himself, far beyond Redwood Sam's death-grip, he saw a thick black fog rolling toward him, and he knew that if he just let that fog keep coming, the pain would soon go away and he could rest. He wanted to rest very much.

Cord felt the cool edges of the fog swirling around his neck like icy fingers, making it hard to breathe. It would be easy now to relax and let it cover him completely like a comforting blanket. But there was a part of Cord Diamondback that understood the black cloud and what it meant. A part that would never give in to it. Would never give in to any beast, man, or supernatural power. He had fought most of his life and, damn it, he would fight now!

He needed to clear his head, drive away that black fog. And there was only one thing that would do that now. Pain. Pure white pain. Suddenly he snapped his head forward, smashing his tender broken cheek into Redwood's forehead. An agonizing jolt of lightning swept away the black fog and any thoughts about rest. Now all he thought about was punishment. And how he would deliver it.

Diamondback reached around with both hands and grabbed fistfulls of greasy black hair at the back of Redwood's neck. He pulled with every bit of strength he had left, ignoring his own pain. Slowly he forced Redwood's head further and further backward. But still the giant wouldn't loosen his iron grip on Cord's spine. The muscles in Redwood's neck stood out like thick miners' rope as he strained against Cord's pull.

When he had finally forced Redwood's head back until the chin tilted toward the roof, Diamondback released one of his hands and jammed his forearm straight down into Redwood's exposed throat.

There was a horrible croaking as Redwood's arms sprang free, dropping Cord to his feet. Redwood's eyes were huge and bulging as he stumbled backwards, struggling to suck in air.

Cord leaped forward, his fists snapping into Redwood's face and body with unending regularity. He battered Redwood relentlessly until his own fists were numb.

By now the crowd was no longer boisterous or cheering. They were silent, reverent. Someone in the back got sick and threw up.

Finally exhausted, Cord loaded everything into a left hook/right cross combination, whipping Redwood Sam's head back and forth like a Pennsylvania Dutch weather vane. Redwood's eyes rolled up into his head as he toppled over with a resounding thud, a big cloud of stable dust enshrouding him.

"End of round three," Deputy Marshal Fenton announced.

Redwood's chubby manager rushed over to his sprawled fighter and dragged him back to his corner. He threw a ladle of water in his face, slapping him repeatedly on the cheeks. When the manager saw how much blood was splattering his own expensive clothes from the slapping, he decided to just shake Redwood by the shoulders.

Cord sank onto his own stool with a sigh, uncertain if he'd ever be able to get up again. His spine felt like a freshly wrung chicken's neck. His arms and legs were marble slabs. With great relief he stared across the ring at Redwood's still-closed eyes.

Then the eyes opened.

A groan of apprehension skimmed through the crowd. They had seen enough for today and were anxious now to get back to the comfort of their routine lives, their safe homes.

Redwood sat up. The dark dried blood smeared around his face made the whites of his eyes seem even whiter, as if he were wearing a strange shade of blackface in a minstrel show.

"Time," Deputy Marshal Fenton said, though much of the previous enthusiasm was gone from his voice. "Toe the mark, boys."

Cord struggled to his feet like a man swimming against spring rapids, aware of how much each step was costing him. He saw the edges of that ominous black cloud seeping toward him again and he shook his head briskly, pushing it away for now. His bruised and swollen fists hung limply at his sides. Finally he reached his mark and waited, reeling dizzily.

Redwood Sam rose from his stool as if defying all natural laws of gravity. He shuffled forward with short awkward steps like a baby learning to walk. His arms seemed to hang past his knees, almost scraping the ground. There was an odd expression on his face, not a grin or a sneer this time, more like a contented smile. He took the last step up to his line.

"Ready?" Deputy Marshal Fenton asked, his arm raised in the air.

Cord nodded.

Redwood Sam said, "Ready," in a dry soft whisper.

Then he pitched face-forward into the dirt.

"Well," Deputy Marshal Fenton said, plucking the

soggy cigar from his mouth and scratching his neck. "I reckon that makes Cord Diamondback here the winner."

A loud roar of jubilation washed through the barn, Cord suspected more from relief that it was all over than from celebration of his victory. These small-town people had never seen a real prizefight before; it would take some time getting over.

Redwood Sam's manager helped Redwood back to his corner, where the two of them stared angrily at Cord, then the crowd, and finally at each other.

"Yahoo!" Jimmy shouted, waving his hat over his head. "I knew you could do it, one hand tied behind your back. Yessir."

Cord winked a painful eye at Jimmy who burst out with another "Yahoo!"

Mathew slipped a firm arm around Cord's waist and hurried him through the crowd, past those trying to slap Cord on the back, and into his combination stockroom and private office. "Close the door, boy," he told Jimmy. He sat Cord down on the old wooden bed and lifted his feet up for him. "Now just lie there awhile."

"Thanks."

Mathew nodded.

"I think this would be a good time to get the prize money from Deputy Marshal Fenton," Cord said.

Mathew cocked his head. "You're the most suspicious man I've ever known. You don't think Fenton would steal it, do you?"

"Probably not. But I've seen it happen before to better men than him. Or somebody might just try to rob him. Anyway, I'd rest better knowing we had the money."

"Okay, Cord. Let's go, Jimmy."

The two of them left, closing the door firmly behind them.

Cord closed his eyes and sighed. Dull pain twisted through every part of his body. Some if it would take weeks to go away, some might never go away at all. But he'd worry about that later. Right now he just wanted to close his eyes and . . .

The door banged open and the pretty girl with the slick gun barged in like someone used to getting her own way. Cord turned his head carefully to face her.

She winced. "Jesus, mister, you're a mess."

"Thanks. Your congratulations are appreciated."

"I didn't mean—"

"What do you want?"

She tilted her hat back and hitched a thumb in her pocket. She wasn't much more than five feet tall, but she gave the impression she could take care of herself, and anyone else she had a mind to.

"Well, my name's Jodi Lawrence, and like I said before, I came here to hire you. I've been riding four whole days!"

"Consider me hired."

She stood there and stared, her mouth half open.

"Anything else?" Cord asked.

"Well, I figured we should get started tonight. It's real important we get where we're going as soon as possible."

"Tomorrow," Cord said, shifting uncomfortably on the hard bed.

"But if we leave now we'll get back half a day sooner."

Cord closed his eyes. "Tomorrow."

"Why goddamn tomorrow?" she yelled, stepping toward Cord. "Why not tonight?"

Cord opened one eye. "I'm afraid of the dark."

She stared at him again, her cheeks flushed with rage, her pale blue eyes darkening like gathering thunderheads. "Don't you at least want to know the details of what you're going to judge?"

Cord opened the other eye. "Tomorrow."

The young woman glared at Cord a long time, then just shook her head sadly. "You ain't like no judge I've ever heard of."

Cord Diamondback closed his eyes and smiled.

3.

"Here, let me do that," she insisted, pushing him back onto her bed. The worn springs groaned as he flopped heavily onto the old mattress.

"I can take care of myself," Cord protested.

"So I see." Amy Simms began unfastening the buttons on the front of his pants, shaking her head and clucking her tongue at him.

"Chrissakes, I can take my own pants off, woman." Cord tried to raise himself to his elbows and rebutton his pants.

She batted away his hands. "You didn't seem to mind me doing this last night."

"That was different."

"It's been 'different' every night we've been together."

He laughed, dropping back onto the bed without a struggle. "You win this round, Amy." He reached over and squeezed the back of her thigh through the rough gingham dress. She slapped away his hand, trying to maintain her severe expression. He squeezed her thigh again, higher this time, and she grinned wickedly.

"Stop it, Cord, or I'll do some squeezing of my own." She hovered over his open pants and nodded at his exposed half-stiff penis.

He laughed again, arching his rump so she could

tug off his blood-splattered pants. She'd already cleaned up his cuts and wounds, and soaked his battered cheek in cold mountain water, bringing the swelling down. Cord had examined the damage in her cracked and chipped mirror and was pleased that the cheek probably had only a minor fracture, one that would heal relatively fast. Provided he stayed out of fights for a few weeks. A hell of a provision, considering his past.

He studied Amy Simms as she fussed over him, folding his pants over the chair, checking the door for the eighth time to make sure it was locked so Jimmy wouldn't barge in unexpectedly. She wasn't a beautiful woman, really, not the kind of beauty that that pesky Jodi Lawrence girl who hired him was. Amy was more handsome than beautiful, he decided, and she had to work at it some just to achieve that much.

Her hair was a dull brown and her eyes a sad grey. The dry winds and harsh sun had tanned her skin against its delicate nature, causing her to look a few years older than her thirty-one years. But she had a gentle style and quick wit, and she made love without shame or false modesty—all of which made Cord Diamondback awfully glad to be in her company. Truth be known, he preferred a good-natured mature woman like Amy to the perky younger girls he usually ran into. He'd gotten to the point where good conversation was as important as good sex.

"Okay, champ," she said, lifting his bare feet onto the bed, "I guess you'll want to change your own shirt."

"Yeah."

"Then I'll check on Jimmy and be back in a minute." She opened her dresser and tossed him a clean white shirt that her husband used to wear at the bank. "It'll be kinda small around the chest, neck,

arms, and waist, but other than that it should fit."
She unlocked the door and stalked out of the room,
the anger in her voice hanging in the air behind her
like stale cigar smoke.

He frowned through his swollen lip as he sat up
and peeled off his sweaty shirt. He didn't blame her
for being annoyed. Certainly it must seem strange to
her that he always wore a shirt, even when they
made love. He'd explained it away at first by telling
her of a sensitive burn he didn't want exposed. In the
beginning she'd been sympathetic. But soon, like
most women, she'd wanted to see it to help him.
He'd refused. Again, she'd been understanding of his
shyness. At first. Then it became a symbol to her of
something he wouldn't share, something he was hiding from her.

And, of course, she'd been right.

Had she seen him without his shirt she too would
have known who he really was, and he couldn't trust
even her not to turn him in to the law. He couldn't
trust anybody anymore.

Amy came through the door, locked it, double-
checked the lock, and walked over to the bed. When
she saw Cord in her husband's shirt she giggled.

"What?" he asked.

"That shirt. It would fit Jimmy better than you."

Cord looked down at himself and laughed too. His
broad chest and hard muscles were straining the seams,
threatening to explode through the shirt. He couldn't
even roll the cuffs above his thick forearms. "Aw,
hell," he said, "put out the lamp."

Amy turned the wick down and blew out what
was left of the flickering flame. The room went black,
except for a pale haze around the window from the
half-moon.

Cord peeled the shirt off his back and lay stretched out on the bed naked and hard. Some of the moonlight etched white ridges, highlighting the rocky curves and flat planes of his long, muscular body.

Amy stopped breathing a moment as she stared at him, something thick like passion caught in her throat. Quickly she stripped off her clothing, stepping out of her plain dress and her best underclothes, which she'd worn especially for him. She stood naked next to the bed, her eyes welling slightly from his gesture of trust. She paused, letting his hungry gaze roam across her body, enjoying his open lust. Her nipples were already budding out, hard and pointed; her full round breasts ached to be touched, kissed.

"Come here," he said softly.

She put her hands on her hips and smiled, but she didn't move.

Cord smiled too. He knew she was pleased because he'd removed his shirt, that she saw it as more than it really was. In fact, he knew it was too dark, even with the slight haze of moonlight, to see his scars clearly. She would be able to feel them when they touched, but she would think of them as the burns he'd mentioned earlier. So there was no real danger here.

She stood next to the bed, her dark pubic hairs less than a foot from his face. He could smell her rich musky odor, sweet and earthy like fresh-plowed soil. His penis throbbed with more blood, straining to grow even bigger, though it could not possibly. Finally he reached out, circled her buttocks with his arm, and pulled her down next to him, burying his face between her legs.

Amy let out a small gasp of pleasure, then spread her legs further. Cord's tongue probed each moist ridge and crevice with gentle insistency. Amy clamped her hands on the back of his head and pulled him deeper while thrusting her hips up to meet his mouth.

"God, Cord," she whispered. "My God!"

Cord continued burrowing, conscious of the sharp pain in his injured cheek where it pressed against her warm thigh. But the pain seemed to excite him even more, like a spur to his back. He felt her sticky wetness drip down his chin and he began lapping her with more urgency, swallowing every drop of her he could. The taste was exotic, like herb-seasoned broth. He started to move faster, trying to match her own panting rhythm. Her left hand pulled his head even closer, until his mouth and chin were pressed into her sopping nest. Her right hand was massaging her own breast, roughly pinching the erect nipple.

"Jesus, yes," she said. She bucked faster and faster, her buttocks bouncing off the bed, her breathing becoming more shallow. Lifting her legs higher, she grabbed her own ankles and pushed them even further apart. She turned her head into the pillow so her cries of passion wouldn't be heard by Jimmy down the hall.

The bed creaked and shook with each movement Cord made, but Amy was too far gone to care. Her wet thighs began to clamp together, her legs straightened and her toes pointed. Muscles flexed through her calves. His tongue slid in and out, then flicked up and down until, with a loud muffled scream into the pillow, her body shuddered and went rigid, then shuttered again. She moaned deeply with each wave, her mouth open gulping air.

Afterwards, it took her a minute or two to regain her breath. Cord stretched out next to her, wrapping his arms around her to keep her warm.

"Jesus, Cord," she sighed, "your cheek."

"It's fine. Best medicine in the world."

With a gentle finger, she lightly traced his jawbone to his chin. "But I wanted to take care of *you*. You're the injured one."

"Don't worry so much. Learn to *receive* pleasure, not just give it."

"That'll take some doing. I haven't had much practice at it, before you." She said it without bitterness about the past, which made Cord hug her closer. A few minutes of silence followed before she asked, "You mad because I didn't go to your fight this afternoon?"

"No. Bare-knuckled fighting isn't for most people. In fact, if I wasn't in the fight, I wouldn't have gone."

She laughed.

He decided this was as good a time as any to tell her what she didn't want to hear. There was never a good time or a good way, so he just told it straight. "Look, Amy, there's no easy way to tell you this, but I'll be leaving Walkers Rest tomorrow."

She stiffened. "For how long?"

He didn't answer.

"Oh." She nodded in the dark.

"I've got a job somewhere."

"Where?"

"I'm not sure. Four days' ride or so.

"What kind of job?"

He hesitated, then said softly, "Judging."

"What?"

"Judging."

"You mean like a rodeo or something?"

"No. People."

She rolled onto one elbow. "I don't get it. You a judge of some kind?"

"Well, not officially. I'm not a federal judge or anything like that. I'm a free-lance judge. An arbitrator, really. Folks that have a disagreement between themselves hire me to settle their dispute."

"That don't make sense. Why don't they just get a real judge?"

"Real judges can take a long time to get to some places. Then when he finally does show up, a court case can take a long time. Some people would rather settle it faster their own way. Also, a lot of people out here don't trust government officials to be fair. That's where I come in."

"I can understand that. Everyone in Walkers Rest knows that the judge we got settled a case in favor of Tom Watkins only two days after attending a fancy dinner party out on the Watkins ranch." She sat up even further, suddenly fascinated with this new revelation. "Who pays you?"

"Both parties involved."

"But what if they don't like your decision? What then?"

"They don't have any choice."

"You mean you make 'em like it?"

He shrugged. "Sometimes."

She studied him with a curious tilt of her head. "That must mean you're kind of a gunman. But you've never even worn a gun since you've been in this town."

"I'm not judging here," he said. "I only wear it when I travel or work."

"Judging, huh? You any good at it?" She laughed. "Never mind, it's a silly question. I know you're good. You're the kind that's good at everything."

He smiled and kissed her shoulder.

"Now hold on there a minute. This is interesting stuff. I want to know more."

Cord slipped a bruised hand between her legs and dipped his finger into her wet flesh. She jumped slightly.

"One more question," he said, easing his finger deeper.

"Oooh, Cord, ahh . . ." She rolled her lower lip between her teeth and arched her back so he could go even deeper. "I can't think . . ."

"Good."

"No, one more question, you said. If you're so good at judging, how come you still fight?"

"There aren't that many judging jobs around. Fighting's just a way for me to pick up some spare cash between jobs. Now that's your last question." He thrust another finger in to the last knuckle.

"Christ," she sighed with pleasure, her hips rotating slightly. "This, ah, this person that hired you today. How'd they know where you were?"

He nibbled her neck. "I run ads in a lot of small rural newspapers, places where a judge might be hard to get. Some word of mouth. I have a friend in San Francisco who I wire where I am from time to time in case someone wants to get in touch with me."

"Who's this friend?" She arched a suspicious eyebrow. "A wife maybe?"

"A friend."

With both hands clutching his wrist, she pulled his hand free from her body and pushed him flat onto his back. "Now it's your turn to relax."

"But—"

"Learn to receive, Cord."

He laughed and followed her advice. And receive

he did. She bent over him, her warm mouth gulping up most of his flagging penis. Almost immediately it was back to its full size, bumping the back of her throat. Amy quickly cupped his balls and gently squeezed. He felt a shock of pleasure scratch across his abdomen.

He could feel her teeth now, gently biting the shaft. Cord opened his eyes and watched as her head bobbed up and down, both hands busily squeezing and probing. A thick drop of her saliva rolled lazily down the shaft. Slowly the pressure began to build until he could feel a warm tingling through his thighs and an aching in his penis. She sensed his need now and her head moved faster, her teeth biting a little harder. His hips thrust to match her rhythm and she slid a hand over him and grabbed a solid buttock. The build-up of pressure felt like a fire climbing his spine. He moved even faster, urging her with his hands clutching her hair.

Finally he exploded into her mouth with a great sigh, his back arched eight inches off the bed. Amy kept swallowing, her mouth still holding him, her hand still cupped around his balls. Almost immediately afterwards, he felt exhausted, as if he'd kicked down his last rail of defense, allowing all the aches and pains he'd accumulated during the fight to begin their systematic throbbing.

Amy stretched out next to him, tugging the covers over both of them. "Sleep," she whispered, burying her face next to his. "Sleep."

He did.

Until the violent pounding on the bedroom door seemed to wake him almost immediately.

4.

Diamondback bolted up out of the bed and grabbed the Winchester .44-.40 that Amy kept propped in the corner next to the bed. He pumped the lever once and swung the barrel around gut-level with the door.

"Get up, Diamondback!" the familiar voice demanded angrily, then thumped the door again with something heavy. "Let's go!"

"Aw, hell," Cord frowned, lowering the rifle.

Amy jumped out of bed and ran toward the door. "Jimmy," she whispered, frightened for her son.

Cord grabbed her arm as she ran by and swung her around. "It's okay, Amy," he said, pulling her close. "Jimmy's fine. Just some fool girl who thinks she's a little tougher than anybody's got a right to be."

It was still dark in the room, with less than two hours having passed since Cord and Amy had drifted off to sleep, legs and arms entwined, their bodies spent with pleasure.

"Do you know what time it is, girl?" Cord shouted through the door.

"Yeah," she snapped. "It's tomorrow."

Cord shook his head and laid the Winchester on the bed. "Toss me my trousers, please."

Amy carried the trousers around the side of the bed. "What's going on here, Cord."

"It's that judging job I was telling you about."

"Now?"

He shrugged. "It must be pretty important for her to bust in here like that. Besides, now that I'm up I don't think I could go back to sleep very easily."

"I could help you," she said, but there was more desperation in her voice than passion. She wanted him to stay.

He said nothing as he reached for his pants.

"I was gonna wash them today. Get some of that blood out."

"I've got another pair in my pack. I'll change on the trail."

The door thumped again. "You coming, Diamond-back?"

"You hit that door once more," Cord said coldly, "and the only place you'll be going is through the window."

The knocking stopped.

Amy went over to her dresser and opened the bottom drawer. She stooped over, rummaged for a few seconds, then pulled out a red flannel collarless shirt. "I bought this for you at Ike's today after I heard you won your fight. Used some of my winnings."

Cord crossed the room and unfolded the shirt. It wasn't fancy, nothing in this small dried up town was, but it was probably the best, most expensive one she could buy here. He slipped in on and buttoned it. "Fits perfect," he lied, hunching slightly so she wouldn't notice where it pulled a little across the chest.

"Really?" she smiled.

"Best shirt I've ever owned."

She shook her head. "No need to dive into the well

after that lie. I figure you've owned a lot fancier shirts than this."

"Fancier, maybe. But not better." He hugged her tight and kissed her full on the lips. She sagged into his arms and kissed him with all her might, as if she were draining some small part of him that might stay with her forever.

He gently nudged Amy away while he pulled on his worn boots and she quickly donned a cotton housecoat. The silence between them was thick with loss, on both sides, but Cord's was mixed with the excitement at what lay ahead.

After they were dressed, Cord opened the bedroom door to reveal an agitated Jodi Lawrence leaning against the wall, her hand resting menacingly on the butt of her gun. "Don't make any more threats to me, Diamondback," she hissed in the half-lit hallway. "I know how to use this gun."

Cord ignored her, turning to watch young Jimmy as he padded sleepily down the hall, knuckling his eyes with his tiny fists. "Mom? Cord? What's going on?"

"Nothing, Jimmy," Cord said. "Just an ill-mannered guest with more brass than brains. We have to pity such folks and treat them kindly."

Jodi Lawrence bared her teeth with a snarl. "Why you big dumb cowboy! How dare you speak about me like that! I'm not some local rube towngirl, you know."

Cord shook his head sadly. "I know. Unfortunately." He turned to face Amy and Jimmy, cutting off Jodi's angry protest. "You two take care now." He put an arm around each and hugged them close.

"Where you going, Cord?" Jimmy asked.

"Got some business to take care of, Jimmy. Your ma will explain."

"You coming back soon?"

Cord noticed the expectancy in Amy's eyes as she waited for him to answer. He would have preferred a lie here, but that just wasn't his way. "Not likely, Jimmy."

Amy's face sagged some, but she managed to keep her smile. Cord had to admit, standing next to this fresh-faced young Jodi Lawrence, Amy looked even older, more worn. The eyes were wrinkled, the mouth bracketed by crevices, the skin a little dry. But somehow with that forced smile and her arm around her sleepy son, she looked to be a hell of a woman, and Cord Diamondback was suddenly very angry at Jodi Lawrence.

He turned and growled at her, "Since you sneaked in on your own, you know the way out. Wait for me outside."

She started to argue, caught the dark look in his eyes, and left quickly.

He gathered up the rest of his gear, strapped on his Smith & Wesson Shofield .45, the gun said to be favored by Jesse James, and strode down the hallway toward the front door. Amy and Jimmy followed close behind.

He stopped at the door, kissed both on the forehead, and left before anybody said something to make it harder.

Jodi was waiting a few feet outside the door, astride her chestnut mustang with a funny straight posture, like someone riding in a show. Cord's brown-and-white dappled appaloosa was saddled and waiting beside her.

"I took the liberty," she explained, nodding at his horse.

Cord strapped on his saddlebags, checked his Winchester .44 rifle to make sure it was fully loaded and that the firing pin was in working condition. He had no reason to like this girl, certainly no reason to trust her.

"Which way?" he said, swinging up into his saddle.

"North of Denver."

Cord tugged the reins, urging his horse south along the main street through Walkers Rest. A few hundred miles to the east, a mist of pale sunlight was seeping up over the edge of the world.

Jodi Lawrence trotted after Cord, trying to keep up with his larger horse's easy lope. "Don't you want to know the details?" she hollered after him, one hand on her hat to keep it from blowing off.

"Later," he said without turning his head.

As they rode through the main street, they passed the Dry Goods & Clothing Store, Hanson's Drug Store, Bartlett's Tin Goods Store, and the Ebony Palace Hotel. All was quiet and still as residents tried to squeeze the last few hours of sleep out of a long hard day that promised to be followed by an endless string of long hard days.

Nothing stirred.

Except for one dark room at the Ebony Palace. Inside that tiny room, standing off to one side of the dirty window, the tall lanky man watched. His thin boney hand with the calloused thumb from cocking the hammer of his revolver a million times a year, swept open the tattered curtain, handsewn by the owner of the Ebony Palace, Sarah Makepeace. He was staring down into the street, studying the two horses heading southbound out of town. He drew out his Remington Frontier .44 and spun the chamber in what had become more of a nervous habit than a sign of caution. He sighed with annoyance as he realized he had yet another hard ride ahead of him. Damn, there were two of them now.

He'd liked it better when there was only the girl to kill.

5.

By the time they'd crossed the Wyoming border into Colorado, Diamondback was certain of two things: the woman he was riding with was about as prickly and tough as cactus stew; and the man that was following them meant business. Jodi Lawrence's nasty manners didn't bother him much, but the rider pinned to his back did. Whoever was tracking them was pretty good for a white man, but apparently too scared of losing them to keep a cautious distance. For someone that good to be that careless bothered Cord. It meant that the tracker was worried, and that meant something important was going on. Deadly important.

"We'll follow Crow Creek a few more miles to where it hooks up to Lone Tree Creek," he told Jodi, pointing past a thicket of juniper trees. "Then we can trace the Goodnight-Loving Cattle Trail for awhile."

"That's not the way I came."

"Yeah, that's why a three-day ride took you four."

She kicked her mustang sharply, urging him to catch up to Cord's appaloosa. "You think you know everything, don't you, Diamondback?"

"Isn't that why you hired me?"

For a fraction of a moment her eyes clouded with two emotions he hadn't seen in her before, vulnerability and confusion. For the first time her voice was low, almost gentle. "Right now I don't know why I hired you."

Cord pulled up his horse near a juniper tree and climbed off. "Well, this looks like as good a spot as any to try to remember. Especially over some boiling hot coffee."

Whatever emotion had been troubling her evaporated without a trace like a drop of water on a hot skillet. Suddenly her voice was cold and bossy again. "We haven't been riding all that long to rest so soon. I can talk while we ride."

"I suspect you can talk any time, but I like to sit down when I have my morning coffee. On something that isn't moving."

She stared at him with eyes as hard as knuckles. But Cord just grinned, turning his back on her while he unfastened the latigo.

"Aw, hell," she spat and hopped off her horse.

Cord uncinched his saddle and pulled it off the appaloosa's back.

"What are you doing that for," she demanded. "They've only been on the road a few hours."

"We have a long ride ahead, and it won't hurt to give them every rest we can now before we start up into the mountains."

She looked startled. "I haven't told you where we're going. What makes you think it's the mountains?"

"Your clothes for one thing. In case you haven't noticed, it's summer around here, yet you're wearing thick woolen clothing." He grinned. "Complete with cotton longjohns I'd guess."

She blushed brightly and sputtered, "I—I'll thank you to mind your own business about my . . . my personal clothing."

Cord ignored her outburst. "Add to it that heavy

fur-lined overcoat you've got strapped to your saddle and I'd say you've come down from some cold mountain air. Since it's near Denver I'd guess the Front Range." He tied his horse to the tree and rustled through his saddlebags for his coffee pot. "If you want some of this coffee you might start gathering some kindling wood."

"I don't think that's such a good idea. What with Indians on the loose and such."

Cord shook his head. "You know much about the Indians around here?"

"I've heard about them," she said defensively. "And read about them."

"Well, then you know we're still a ways from the Arapaho reservation. Besides, they've been pretty calm since the Sand Creek Massacre back in '64. I suspect Little Raven's word is still good. And since Dull Knife's Cheyennes have been captured at Fort Robinson, we should be relatively safe."

"Naturally *you'd* say that."

"What's that supposed to mean?"

"Well, you'd have to defend them, what with your Indian name and all."

"What makes you think it's Indian?"

"C'mon, with a name like yours. *Diamondback.* I just thought . . ." She looked confused. "Isn't it Indian?"

He smiled and pointed to a nearby tree. "Looks like some good kindling wood over there."

Jodi started to say something, stopped, shook her head angrily, and stomped over to the tree and began gathering wood.

Once the small fire was built and the two of them were sipping coffee and gnawing jerky, Diamondback leaned against the juniper tree and sighed. "That's damn good coffee, I must admit."

"You made it."

He smiled. "That's why I must admit it."

She sipped her coffee. "You aren't at all what I expected."

"What'd you expect?"

"I don't know. Someone more . . . official, I guess. Proper. You know, dark suit and preacher's hat. Fancy words. Like a real judge."

"If you want a real judge it's not too late."

"If I could've gone to a real judge I would have. But no real judge would have anything to do with what I've got in mind." She waited for Cord to comment. When he didn't, she continued. "You're just, well, different. I don't mean that nasty. It's just that you have a reputation. Even back East some people have heard of you. Yet you were standing in the middle of a livery barn exchanging punches with some hairy ape. Somehow that just lacks, uh . . ."

"Dignity?"

"Well, yeah, I guess. You being a judge and all, even a private one. Why do you do it?"

Cord threw the last few drops of coffee over his shoulder and refilled his cup. "Money. I may have some reputation, helped no doubt by the exaggerations of magazine and newspaper writers crawling all over us out here, but a reputation doesn't feed me all the time. Besides, you overestimate my fame. Not one person in Walkers Rest knew the name Cord Diamondback."

"Hell, those ignorant farmers wouldn't recognize President Hayes' name."

Cord gazed at her over his cup, curious at the

hostility and contempt in her voice when she spoke about the people of Walkers Rest.

"You from around here?" he asked.

"No, I told you, north of Denver."

"I don't mean now. I mean born and raised."

"What business is that of yours?"

He shrugged. "None."

"That's right." She lowered her eyes and stared into her coffee cup. After a minute of silence she mumbled, "Kansas."

"Nice state."

She laughed a harsh humorless laugh. "Hardly. It's a God-forsaken hole filled with the same ignorant types we just left. When I was younger I used to think it was really hell and that God sent all the misfits and losers there to live for eternity as punishment."

"Your parents farmers?"

The same harsh laugh scraped her throat. "Not just farmers, but the biggest, wealthiest in the county."

"That explains it," Cord nodded.

"Explains what?"

"Why you ride and speak that way."

She straightened her back defensively. "What's that supposed to mean? What way?"

"Well, you ride awfully stiff, as if you're used to riding an English saddle. And you talk like you've had some education, more than you'd get in a Kansas one-room. I figure you've spent a few years in some Eastern school somewhere."

"Washington," she said smugly. "The capital."

"Of course," he smiled. "And I'd bet you were quite the toast of the town. Running around to important parties and diplomatic functions."

"I was considered amusing company in certain circles."

"What happened? How'd the queen of the capital end up squatting next to Crow Creek, wearing man's clothing and keeping company with a brute like me?"

She jumped to her feet and tossed what was left of her coffee into the fire. It sizzled, like her eyes. "You're making fun of me."

"No, I'm not. I'm just curious about who I work for."

"What difference does that make. I haven't even told you what the job is yet. Don't you ever want to know?"

"First things first." He calmly stared into her angry face. "What happened in Kansas?"

She hesitated, still glaring at him. Finally she just sighed and sat back down. "My little brother died. Milking sickness."

Cord nodded sympathetically. He'd heard it called by many different names, puking fever, swamp sickness, the trembles. But whatever the name, it was a horrible way to die, stiff and sore and vomiting for days. They say it was caused by drinking milk or eating butter taken from a cow poisoned by grazing on the leaves of the white snakeroot or rayless goldenrod plants. He knew that President Lincoln's mother had died of it when little Abraham was only nine. And Cord had witnessed a few fatal cases of it himself over the years.

"Anyway, he was only eleven when they buried him and sent for me to come back from Washington. Then they tried to bury me too."

"Bury you?"

"Smother is a better word."

"Too much love?" Cord said.

"Too much of everything. After losing Curtis they were so scared something would happen to me, they wouldn't let me out of their sight for a minute. It was like I was in jail. Not that there was anyplace to go or anyone but dung herders to see, not with all those dumb farmer boys used to fiddling the privates of their heifers and sheep."

"They didn't appreciate a real lady."

"You're making fun of me again."

"Maybe a little. But you should try laughing at yourself every once in awhile. Then you wouldn't act so spoiled all the time."

"Spoiled!" She glared at Cord for a minute, her eyes raking him to the bone. "It doesn't matter what you think anyway. I hired you to do some judging, but not of me. Now, you interested in the job or not?"

"If I wasn't interested I wouldn't be here having such a fun time, would I?"

Jodi sat back down, crossing her legs and adjusting her gun where it pressed into her side. "I know you're supposed to be good with that gun. That's what I read, anyway."

"Where'd you read that?"

"In Washington. A magazine ran an article about you once. It was one of those 'wild West' magazines, the kind we weren't allowed to have at the school. One of the girls sneaked it in among her petticoats. Of course, they described you as being much taller."

"They describe everybody out here as being taller," Cord said.

"Well, it doesn't matter how tall you are. As long as you're as good with that gun as they claimed. You'll need to be for this job. If you want to come out of it alive."

"Sounds serious."

"It is. I want you to settle a disagreement between some people and my man."

"Your man?" he smiled.

"My *lover*," she flared defiantly. "Maybe you've heard of him. Victor Curry."

Cord's face was suddenly very grim. He leaned forward. " 'Angel Eyes' Curry?"

She smiled, pleased that she'd finally gotten a reaction. "That's him. So you have heard of him?"

There weren't many people in the mid-West who hadn't heard of the young man who tortured his own father and older brother to death with a branding iron.

"Well," Diamondback said coldly. "You've got my attention."

6.

She held the small wooden box carefully, reverently, as if she feared whatever was inside might leap out at her and attack. Slowly, with painful gentleness, she opened the hinged lid. Turning her head away with disgust, she thrust it under Cord's nose.

He glanced down, keeping his face calm, but swallowing something bitter at the back of his throat.

It was a severed human ear!

The smell was the worst part, for it was shrivelled and black from decomposing. Whoever had done the cutting hadn't been particularly sensitive, or sober, for it looked as if it had been hacked off after several false starts.

"Now do you believe me?" she said, slamming the lid closed and fumbling to lock the metal clasp.

"I believed you before. Showing me his ear was your idea."

"I wanted to make sure you believed me."

"No you didn't. You wanted to justify what he's doing right now."

"Maybe," she said softly, that hint of vulnerability creeping in again. Then it was gone without a trace, like a shooting star that burned itself out. "But it doesn't matter why. You know what I want you to do."

Cord took off his hat, wiped the sweat from his forehead with his sleeve, and shook his head with a mighty sigh. "Let me make sure I've got the facts right so far."

She groaned. "We've already been over it."

"Indulge me. I'm a slow learner."

"Christ."

"Now, you've been riding with Victor 'Angel Eyes' Curry for almost four months now, right?"

She nodded.

"How exactly did you hook up with someone like him?"

"I don't see where that's any of—"

"Just tell me," Cord barked.

She looked startled at his anger, and replied quickly. "In Kansas. I'd managed to get away from my parents long enough to go roller skating at the town rink. Vic and his cousin Ray were there too." She smiled at the memory. "Vic could hardly stand up. Ray had to hold him up by the back of his trousers."

"Did you know who he was when you took up with him?"

"Sure. He told me right away." She paused, thinking back. "Well, almost right away. A week later, after we'd, uh, you know."

"Had sex."

"Made love!" she retorted, flushing a deep crimson. "He told me all about what people said he'd done back in Missouri. But he'd explained how it wasn't like that at all. He didn't do it. It was a couple of drifters. They tortured Vic's brother and pa hoping they'd find out where the old skinflint hid his money. Everybody in those parts knew he was a real miser who didn't trust banks."

"Why didn't Victor tell folks what really happened?"

"He was ashamed. He'd hidden himself under the porch the whole time and watched as those filthy animals branded his pa and brother over and over again. He listened to their screams of agony for hours before they finally died. And when it was all over he ran away because he didn't want people to know he'd hidden out. You have to remember, that was five years ago and he wasn't much more than a boy then. Only seventeen. And he's been on the run ever since."

Cord nodded at the wooden box with the human ear. "And he's been a model citizen ever since?"

"If he'd have been given half a chance, maybe. But they've been hunting him for so long he's had to live as best he could. Robbing sometimes."

"Killing sometimes."

"If he has to," she said coldly. "He hasn't been left much choice. Hell, you wouldn't understand."

Diamondback said nothing, his lips pressed thin into a hard flat line. He thought about his own past for a moment, and what Jodi would say if he told her his real name. Showed her the markings on his back. If she knew that the rewards on him totaled to more than five times what her boyfriend was worth.

"I don't see where all this is getting us," she said. "It doesn't have anything to do with what I hired you to decide."

"Like any good judge, I like to take everything into consideration before I make a ruling. Contributing factors. Now, why did you take up with him?"

She shrugged. "I love him."

"And he was leaving Kansas, which would take you far away from your parents and their over-protectiveness."

"Yeah, that helped."

"Okay, that's the background. Now comes the part that's hard to understand." He pointed at the box with the severed ear. "What the hell happened up in the mountains."

"Well, like I said before, Vic and his gang hadn't been doing so well lately. Bigger banks, faster trains, everything changing so much they couldn't seem to get ahead. Finally one night most of the gang just up and quit. Vic took that real hard, kept blaming himself for being a bad leader. Anyway, he heard there was still plenty of room for prospecting up in the Front Range, so the two of us and his cousin Ray started a placer claim in the foothills up near Dog Trail."

"Any of you ever do any mining before?"

"Ray had done a little. He had this guidebook by some guy named Oakes that told all about how to do it."

Cord shook his head with a wry smile. " *'Here lies the body of D.C. Oakes/Killed for aiding the Pike's Peak hoax.'* You ever hear that before?"

"No. What's that mean?"

"A lot of prospector's used to make dummy tombstones and scratch that little verse on it. Seems Mr. D.C. Oakes was a bit more optimistic about people's chances at mining than the facts called for. Lots of his readers died finding that out."

"Well, we did okay," she huffed proudly.

"How okay?"

"We hauled out almost fifty dollars a day for each of us in less than a week."

"And that's when the trouble started?"

"Yes. A bunch of miners claimed we were stealing from their claims. They tarred and feathered Ray and were going to do the same to Vic, but he pulled his gun and shot one in the leg. He can be pretty hot-headed sometimes."

"So they cut off his ear."

She nodded.

"That's not too unusual. Miner's justice is swift."

"You call cutting a man's ear off justice?"

"Did he steal from the other claims?"

"No! We mined it all ourselves. I thought we were so lucky, that finally our running was through. Every time I sifted another load and saw that gold winking and sparkling in the sun, I knew we were closer to settling down. Buying a house, maybe, or a store somewhere."

"He still had his past to contend with."

"Hell, with enough money you can buy back your past."

"Maybe," Cord said. "But it didn't work out that way for you this time. When did the miners jump you?"

"Right after Vic and Ray came back from town. They'd had our gold assayed at the saloon."

"What happened after they hacked off his ear?"

"They ran us out of town strapped to the backs of smelly old mules." She spoke with a hatred so pure and intense, the words seemed to vibrate with energy. "I tended to Vic's wound and Ray went about scraping himself clean. After that night Vic talked of nothing but going back to Dog Trail and getting revenge and our gold. I think the gold was just the excuse, revenge was what he really wanted. It took us a few weeks, but finally he tracked down some of his old gang and promised them whatever they wanted if they'd ride back with him to get even. Well, a couple of the boys had already joined up with the Tom Delancy Bunch out of the Dakotas. But times haven't been so good for them lately either, so Vic convinced the whole bunch to come along. That made them nearly fifteen strong as we rode back toward Dog Trail. On the way we ran into the Quinn brothers, Ulysses and Jason, and they joined up."

"The Quinns from Texas?"

"Yeah. After that, everything was easy. We rode into Dog Trail and took over the town with hardly a shot. We've been there ever since."

"How long's that?"

"About two weeks."

Cord stretched his arms over his head and yawned. "Sounds like you all got what you want. What do you need me for?"

Jodi leaned forward, that look of vulnerability back in her eyes, the one she always tried to hide. "Between the three outlaw gangs, they've pretty much terrorized the town. They've looted just about everything they could. And they're doing some things that are just downright unspeakable."

"Like what?"

"Well, they've got some of the miners fighting each other while they bet on the winner."

"You mean like boxing?"

"No. Fighting with knives or axes. And I mean to the death. Like those Roman gladiators or something." She took a deep breath and sighed wearily. "Now they've even started to argue amongst themselves over who gets to keep what from all the stuff they've looted. That's where you come in. I want you to figure out a fair split so that everybody is happy. The sooner the better. Maybe then we can all just ride out of there for good."

Cord threw back his head and laughed long and loud.

"What's so damn funny," she shouted angrily.

"You. I mean, what makes you think they'd listen to me in the first place. All the involved parties have to agree that my ruling is binding before I can arbitrate. These boys don't sound like the agreeable type."

"I don't know. I figured you could talk them into it. That's what you do, isn't it?"

"How long were you in Washington?"

"Six years."

"And how long have you been back out here?"

"Nearly eight months."

"You've got some remembering to do about how things are done out here. I would have thought what those miners did to your boyfriend would have been enough to remind you."

"Look, Diamondback, if you were afraid the job would be too tough you should have let me explain it back in Walkers Rest. Instead you had to play the tough cowboy who doesn't need any details. Well, now you've come this far and you owe it to me to see it through. You made a, uh, contract with me."

"You learn about contracts in Washington?"

"Yes, I did."

He shrugged helplessly. "Well, then I guess you've got me. I'll tag along a little further to see what develops."

"That doesn't sound too encouraging."

"It'll have to do." Cord glanced up into the sun. He'd given whoever was following them plenty of time to settle in and get comfortable, and maybe a little careless. There were a few things about the young woman's story that didn't wash clean, but he was used to getting lied to by his clients.

Yet this case was strange in other ways. Never before had he been hired to help several gangs of warring outlaws divide their loot. Particularly ones as brutal as these. And if he didn't play it exactly right, it would be the last time he'd be hired to do anything.

But first he had to do something about the man tailing them. Something sure and final. Something right now.

7.

"It looks dangerous," she said.

"It is."

"You sure you know what you're doing?"

Cord didn't answer. He cinched the saddle tight around his appaloosa and handed the rein of the hackamore headstall to Jodi.

She climbed up onto her mustang. "How far do you want me to ride?"

"Not far," he said, kicking dirt on the ashes of the fire and spreading the burned wood to make sure everything was extinguished. "Keep riding through these trees, weaving in and out so that you're never fully in sight. That ought to bring him closer."

"Who is it do you think?"

"Thought maybe you could tell me."

She shrugged. "How should I know? Can't be one of Vic's men. I left him a note explaining that I was aiming to hire you."

Cord looked surprised. "How'd you know I was in the area?"

"I didn't at first, not till after I telegraphed San Francisco."

"What would you have done if I wasn't within riding distance?"

"Hired someone else, of course. You aren't the only one of your profession, you know."

Diamondback reached up and grabbed a low branch of the juniper tree. With one tug he swung his legs up into the tree until he was squatting among the green awl-shaped leaves. Slowly he climbed higher until he was relatively obscured by the full blooming branches.

"How's this?" he called down.

"Since you asked, it looks silly. There's no need to be so melodramatic. I don't think we're being followed. Even if someone is out there it's probably a coincidence."

"And if it's not?"

She nibbled on her lower lip. "Then it's probably someone out of *your* past." She grinned wryly. "A dissatisfied client perhaps."

That possibility had occurred to Cord too. It wouldn't be the first time someone had come sniffing after him, asking folks about a husky man with a strange pattern of scars on his back. Someone who'd not been fooled by his clean-shaven face or name change. Someone who'd tracked Cord down following some obscure clue he wasn't even aware he'd left behind. Well, if that was so, he'd need to know that too.

Cord hunkered down until his butt grazed the heels of his stovepipe boots, his hands grasping the flimsy end of an overhead branch for balance.

"Go ahead," he told Jodi. "And keep my horse on your right, where he can't be seen clearly through the trees. After you've ridden a couple miles turn around and come back. It'll be all over by then. One way or the other."

She started to say something, her face frowning with concern. But she didn't.

He wasn't surprised. Since he'd gotten to know her he noticed how quickly she brushed away any painful emotions as easily as trail dust. She gave her mustang a nudge in the ribs and rode off, Cord's huge appaloosa tagging along beside her.

Cord waited, his breathing shallow, his muscles tensed for action. If there was one thing he had plenty of it was patience. He'd learned the necessity of that on his first whaling voyage, as a jittery teen-ager perched high above the ship's deck in a tiny crow's nest, waiting for hours for the faintest sign of a whale. Now he used that same patience in hunting men.

It didn't take long.

Within ten minutes he heard the soft clomping and snorting of a husky horse as it picked its way through the trees. Cord slipped the rawhide loop on his holster over the hammer spur of his .45. It wouldn't do for the gun to shake loose at the wrong moment and go tumbling to the ground. He'd seen more than one man gut-shot from a dropped pistol.

The horse snorted again and Cord knew it was almost time. He took a deep breath, his nostrils stinging slightly from the spicy aroma of the juniper berries.

Looking straight down at the fifteen-foot drop to the ground, Cord waited quietly as the clip-clop grew closer. The rider was in no hurry, content to follow the easy tracks Cord had left for him.

Diamondback held his breath, lifted onto his toes, and when he saw the big roan edge into his sight, he grabbed the end of the branch overhead and jumped.

8.

"Shit!" the rider spat as he screwed his head around and up to see what that rustling noise behind him was. His pistol was already half out of its holster.

But that's as far as it got.

Diamondback, clutching the end of a flimsy branch to slow his fall, plummeted toward him with both feet splayed out like battering rams. The horse spooked, jumping back onto its hind legs, and lifting its frightened rider closer to Cord.

"Oomph," the rider cried as Cord's heavy boots struck him in the left shoulder, propelling him over the horse's neck. He somersaulted once before thudding into the ground, where he continued tumbling until he whacked into the trunk of a juniper tree.

When his own feet grazed the ground, Cord released the skinny branch, which flapped back up into the tree like an escaping bird.

The rider was slightly stunned, but his calloused right hand slapped his .44 out of its holster with an instinct that didn't require complete consciousness. He was still trying to shake the dizziness when he opened fire on Cord.

The first bullet dug into the ground less than six inches from where Cord had dropped, kicking a spray of dirt over the square toe of Cord's boot. Cord didn't wait for the next shot. He lunged toward the shaky gunman, his fists cocked like a steam drill. He ignored the temptation to pull his own .45. He wanted information, not a corpse.

The tall skinny rider was working his way to his wobbly feet by inching his back up against the tree trunk. One hand grasped his throbbing head while the other leveled the gun at Cord's charging body.

But too late.

Diamondback drove his shoulder into the gunman's hand, slamming it against the stranger's bony chest. The hand sprang open, knocking the pistol three feet clear of both of them. But the rider fought back, his thin bloodless lips curled into a rodent's snarl. With one hand he clawed at Cord's face, trying to poke his thumbs into Cord's eyes. With his other hand he grabbed for the hunting knife looped onto his gunbelt, fumbling to free the eight inches of tempered steel. Cord batted away the clawed hand and quickly snapped half a dozen solid jabs into his face. The dazed man's head cracked into the tree trunk, chipping away a hunk of bark. Suddenly his legs buckled and he sagged down the length of the trunk, his gunbelt scraping bark all the way down.

"Wha . . . wha . . . ," he mumbled, holding his jaw.

Cord snagged the rider's gun from the ground and swung it toward his chest. Behind him he heard the pounding of hooves. He glanced over his shoulder at Jodi and the two horses as they galloped closer.

"Damn it, woman, I told you to ride a couple miles. You couldn't have gone even one."

"I was worried," she said softly as she hopped off the horse. There it was again, that silvery edge of concern and vulnerability. But again she shrugged it off quickly, forcing her voice to gruffness. "After all, I hired you for a job, not bushwacking passersby."

"This isn't a passerby," Cord said. "Are you, mister?"

The rider was tall, tall even sitting down. But he was so thin that he resembled more a series of folding bones than a flesh-and-blood man. The ridges of his cheeks looked sharp as they protruded against taut grey skin. Thin blue veins webbed visibly at each temple. His eyes were sunken so deep into his face that it was hard to tell their color.

"You mind?" the rider asked, nodding at his hat which laid a foot away.

"Go ahead," Cord said.

The rider's long thin fingers spidered across the ground, snatched the Montana peak hat, brushed off the dirt, poked at the dents, and pulled it low over his forehead. He looked up at Cord with a grim smile. "You mind telling me just what you want, Slick, 'cause I don't have no money worth getting killed over."

"Then we'll try information."

"Don't have much've that, neither." He flashed a row of tiny square teeth, the kind Cord had seen on certain types of fish. Scavenger teeth.

"Then you're luck has just run out." Cord cocked the hammer and pointed it at the rider's left knee. "What's your name?"

"Now, see here, Slick, I don't—"

Diamondback squeezed the trigger. The rider's knee exploded in an eruption of blood and chips of bone. The ragged hole in his pants bubbled with blood. He screamed in agony, grasping his shredded knee.

"My God!" Jodi gasped, holding the horses' reins as they shied from the sudden explosion.

"Jesus Christ and hellfire!" the rider hollered. "Christ, look what you done here, boy. My God, just look!"

Thick syrupy blood was oozing from the wound, seeping between his boney fingers like a dark wine. The rider rocked back and forth, pressing his dusty red bandanna over the hole.

Cord cocked the hammer again and aimed it at the gunman's left arm.

The skinny rider waved a bloody hand of protest. "Cummings, for Chrissake. Red Cummings."

"My God, Diamondback," Jodi whispered. "You just shot that man for no reason."

Cord ignored her. "Why do they call you Red. Your hair's blacker than a crow's ass."

"My daddy's name was Red, so they called me Red too."

"Okay. Next question: why are you following us?"

"Hell, I ain't following you. I ain't following nobody."

Cord pulled the trigger again. The gun jumped, and a big .44 slug gouged out a fleshy chunk of Red Cumming's left arm, just below the shoulder. Cummings slammed back into the tree, screaming from the pain.

Jodi released the snorting horses and rushed forward. "Stop it! Have you gone crazy?" She lunged for Cord's gun.

He grabbed her by the hand, bending it at the wrist. She gave out a high-pitched gasp and dropped to her knees.

"Ooww!" she whined.

"Stay out of this," he told her, still applying enough pressure to keep her on her knees.

"You're crazy!" she screamed. "*Crazy!*"

Diamondback continued, his voice icy calm, his gun hand steady as it pointed at Cummings' other kneecap. "I'll ask you again, Red. Why are you following us? And let me remind you that you're running out of non-vital parts."

Cummings writhed against the tree, fixing a hateful stare on Cord. His thin grey lips were twisted into a threatening scowl. "If I ever get out of this—"

Cord cocked the hammer.

"It was her!" he offered quickly. "I was following her."

"Me?" Jodi gasped.

"Why her?"

Cummings hesitated, looking at his wounds. "Help me with my arm and knee first. Then I'll talk."

Cord pointed the barrel at Cummings' stomach. "A bullet placed in just the right place in your gut will keep you alive for a long time. In a couple hours you'll talk just so I *will* shoot you."

Cummings stared into Cord's flinty eyes, searching for how far this man would actually go. He decided Cord was probably good for his word.

"All right," he winced. "Just give me a chance to catch my breath."

"Suit yourself," Cord shrugged, aiming the pistol at Cummings' good knee and started to squeeze the trigger.

"*Reward!*" Cummings screamed. "I'm after the reward!"

"There's no reward on me," Jodi said.

"Not on you. On 'Angel Eyes ' Curry. I tracked you both across Kansas and into Colorado. I lost your trail up in the mountains when I got word he was getting his old bunch together again up in Nebraska. By the time I caught up with you all, you'd made your way back into Colorado. I was getting supplies in Denver when I saw you ride into the telegraph office. I been on you ever since, figuring you'd lead me to 'Angel Eyes' and his gang."

"Bounty hunter?" Cord asked.

"Yeah, now and then."

"Where you from?"

"Montana." He pointed at his hat, but the movement caused a sudden stab of pain in his wounded arm. "How's about doing me right with some tending to?"

Diamondback was about to respond when a rifle shot cracked the air. He spun around just in time to hear Jodi cry out and see her knocked off her feet. Her eyes were closed before she struck the ground and blood etched a lightening bolt pattern down her face.

Then came the second shot.

9.

"Am I dead?"

Cord laughed. "Not yet."

Jodi tried to lift her head but he gently held her down.

"Don't move yet. Give your brain a chance to adjust."

She nodded, winced at the pain the movement caused, and let her eyes roam around to take in her strange new surroundings. When they came across the dead scalped body sprawled three feet away, she jumped. "My God, it's . . . it's . . ."

"Red Cummings," Cord said. "Been dead most of the day." He reached over and swatted away a flurry of buzzing flies picking hungrily at the crusted scab where Red's hair used to be.

"They scalped him!"

"Yeah, they did. A rather neat job of it too."

Jodi propped herself onto her elbows, her head groggy from pain and shock. She lifted her fingers to her forehead and gingerly dabbed the wound where the bullet had scraped away her skin. Then she looked around, realizing for the first time that they were in an Indian tipi. "What's going on?"

"Right now they're trying to decide whether we should follow Red's example."

"You mean they might kill us?"

"It's possible."

"*And scalp us?*"

"It's possible."

She sat up even straighter, her head throbbing. "My God, who are they? What happened? You said the Arapaho's wouldn't bother us."

"They aren't Arapahos, they're *Ocheti Sakowin*."

"Sioux."

Cord nodded. "But for now I'd stick to the term they prefer. They aren't too fond of anything from the white world right now, even a bastardized term like Sioux."

"Considering our position here, what the hell's the difference."

"Words are very important to Indians, that's why they use them so sparingly. Right now they're trying to decide whether or not to slice the tops of our heads off. The wrong word or improper gesture could insult them. No need to tell you how that might influence their decision. Understand?"

Jodi swallowed, fear draining her face pale. "Yes."

"Good. If you can't remember *Ocheti Sakowin*, use the term *dak-kota*. It means 'council of friends' and they'll appreciate the effort."

"Just like Dakota?"

"Right. Now, these aren't just ordinary Sioux, they're Tetons, and they've got a reason to be damned mad at whites right now. Half of them followed Sitting Bull up to Canada after the defeat at Slim Buttes. These are the same people that owned a 6,000 square-mile gulp of land in the Black Hills. A couple years ago there was a lot of pressure on the government to open up that land for prospectors, and they offered the Tetons six million dollars for the land. Hell, all these people know is buffalos, so they refused the money. But with the buffalo nearly all gone, they had to give up their land the next fall just to get their rightful allotment of winter provisions. Now they have nothing. No money, no land, no buffalo. You can see why they're a little riled."

"But we didn't have anything to do with that. Nor did Cummings there."

"Cummings had made his own mistake. I figured he was lying after he told us that story about him coming from Montana. He was riding a skinny Texas square-rigged saddle with a double cinch. By itself that might not mean anything, but this helps." Cord pulled out a folded piece of paper from his shirt and shook the paper open. He showed the sketch to Jodi, whose eyes widened.

"It's Vic."

"Sure is." He began to read from the wanted poster. "Victor 'Angel Eyes' Curry wanted for Murder, Arson, Cattle Rustling. $500 Reward to any person or persons who will capture and deliver him to any sheriff of Texas. Satisfactory proof of identity will be required."

"Texas?" Jodi said softly, then swooned, collapsing flat onto her back.

"Take it easy now. Take it easy." He bent over her and rubbed a thick salve into her wound. "This will help."

"What is it?"

"It's made from yarrow blossoms for cuts and bruises. Your lucky their medicine man is so modern. This remedy comes from the Utes. He's also given you some powder from the Indian turnip, an old Pawnee remedy for headaches."

She angrily brushed away his hands. "I don't care about that now. Where'd you get that poster?"

"Off our buddy Red Cummings. Though his Christian name was Virgil. Seems he was a bounty hunter all right, but from Texas, not Montana."

"Why would he lie about that?"

"I don't know." Cord smiled. "Interesting, huh?"

"Is that all you can say? 'Interesting.' First, we're followed by a bounty hunter and now we're prisoners of marauding Sioux who might kill us. Oh God, it's all so confusing."

"Not to Red. One of the suspicious things about our shifty friend was that he was riding a Texas saddle but didn't have a cowboy bridle. He had an Indian war bridle, which is nothing more than a length of rope with a lark's-head knot tightened around the horse's jaw. That didn't sit right with me. But just as I was about to ask him about it, the shooting started. The first shot nipped you and the second one drilled him clean through the heart."

"What did you do?"

"I tossed my gun away and threw my hands up as high as they'd go."

She lifted herself back to her elbows, her face reddening with rage. "You mean that's why we're in this fix? You didn't even try to fight them off? What kind of man are you?"

He smiled. "A living one."

"You threw away our chance to escape."

"Lady, there are forty warriors out there, any one of whom could have killed me before I'd have fired one shot. They weren't after us, they were after that son of a bitch for clubbing one of their kids and stealing his horse."

"You mean that's all he did, steal a horse, and they killed and scalped him for that?"

Cord sighed impatiently. "Apparently there's a lot you didn't read in those Washington books about Indians. Especially the part about horses. Indians have an almost religious awe for these animals. The Comanches call it 'god dog.' The Sioux call it 'medicine dog.' Besides, they've had enough stolen from them to make any offense by a white man punishable by death. The only thing they're trying to decide now is whether or not we were friends of his."

"Couldn't they tell we weren't after all the holes you blasted in him?" Her voice was sharp with accusation.

"That's in our favor. But they don't like to jump to conclusions. Also, something like this breaks up their day and gives them a chance to smoke a little and chat."

Jodi stared at the limp corpse of Red Cummings, her face thoughtful and distant. She gazed at the fat flies lazily circling his face like tiny crows.

Cord watched her face for a minute before speaking. "He didn't tell you, did he?"

It took her a couple seconds to react to Cord's voice. "Who?"

"Vic. He didn't tell you about Texas."

She started to bark out an angry, defensive reply, but cut herself off. "No."

Diamondback refolded the poster and shoved it inside his shirt. "There's probably more he didn't tell you."

"Maybe," she said. "But so what? I knew what kind of life he lead when I hooked up with him. I'm not surprised he didn't tell me everything about his past; he's very sensitive about it. Ashamed, really.

Something you wouldn't understand. Besides, I didn't tell him everything about my past either." She tilted her head with a curious frown. "Answer a question?"

"Try me."

"How could you shoot him like that?" She hooked a thumb toward Cummings' corpse. "I mean piece by piece."

"I wanted information."

"Don't you care how you get it, for God's sake?"

"No."

"But you didn't know for sure he was following us."

"I knew."

"Not for sure, you didn't. You couldn't have."

His face was cold, impassive. "I knew."

She stared at him and shook her head. "They named you right, Diamondback."

They sat in silence while Cord considered their predicament. There wasn't much he could do right now but wait. They were both unarmed while outside the tipi was a whole tribe of angry warriors. Their only hope was that the council of elders would recognize that Cummings had also been their enemy. In the meantime, he had to divert Jodi's attention from her own morose thoughts of death, torture, and her lover's secrets. He wanted her in strong spirits when and if they had a chance to escape.

"Look at that," he said, pointing to the far corner.

The buffalo-skin tipi was fairly dark without a fire in the middle. Jodi squinted and followed Cord's pointing finger. "What is it?"

"Juniper berries. While the braves were tracking Cummings, the women gathered juniper berries."

"What for?"

"Lots of uses. To flavor food for one, it gets rid of

the gamey taste in venison. Or to make medicine.
But mostly for alcohol. In fact, that's where the word
gin comes from, the French for juniper, *genièvre*."

She looked at Cord with wonder. "Where do you
get all this stuff you know?"

He laughed. "Plants interest me."

"No. You went to school, didn't you. A real uni-
versity or something."

He couldn't tell her yes, couldn't describe his teen-
age years at sea or the studious years at Harvard
before the deadly incident that changed everything.
Anything he said could be a clue that she might
casually mention to the wrong person, and that would
be enough to hang him.

Suddenly the door flap snapped open and a scowling painted face ducked into the tipi. The young
warrior had Cord's .45 tucked into his waistband
next to his knife. He held up his hands, made them
into fists, and swiveled them back and forth.

"What's he doing?" Jodi asked.

Cord rose to his feet and pulled Jodi up after him.
"The council wants to see us. They've reached a
decision."

"Jesus," Jodi said, swallowing hard. "Judgment
Day."

10.

Cord grabbed her shoulder and tilted her face up toward his. "Do you want to live?"

"Yes, of course."

"Then follow my instructions without hesitation or question. Tetons don't like women to speak out of turn."

Her eyes flared. "Well, they can just—"

He laid a calming hand on her arm. "Remember Red Cummings."

Jodi nodded and fell quiet next to Cord as they approached the Teton council's tipi. This was as close as she'd ever been to a real tipi. As a child she'd seen some Pawnee and Iowa Indians as they traveled across her pa's land, but she'd never been this close to them, close enough to smell their homes and feel their hate. Once in Washington a Senator's aide had taken her to a Wild West Show, but the Indians there seemed pale and indifferent. This was the real thing, a people aching with pride and stinging from humiliation. So far she'd been treated politely, but there was a threatening undercurrent of danger that both frightened and exhilarated her. She was glad to be in Cord Diamondback's company, despite some of the things he'd done. Or maybe, she wondered, because of it.

"It's so smokey," she complained, waving the air in front of her face. Indeed the smoke pouring out of the tops of the many tipis caused a hazy thickness to the air, as if a heavy harbor fog were rolling in.

"Indians can stand smoke a lot better than us," he explained. "They love it. It has religious significance for them."

"Does *everything* have religious significance to Indians?"

"Just about."

They stopped in front of the tipi and the young Indian brave ducked through the open flap, closing it behind him. Jodi started to follow, but Cord grabbed her arm and jerked her back next to him.

"Once the flap's closed we have to be invited in."

"Well, hell, they brought us here, didn't they? What do they expect?"

"They want to test our manners, see how civilized we are."

"Civilized! Of all the . . ."

"Relax. We're lucky. Unlike whites, they're willing to judge each of us as individuals rather than guilt through association. So let's show them our stuff. Ready?"

Jodi took a deep breath and smiled weakly. "Ready."

The flap spanked open and the same young warrior stepped out, waving for them to enter.

Jodi started through but Cord cut her off and entered first. "Men first," he whispered to her. "Once inside, I'll go to the right and you'll go to the left. Remain standing until you're invited to sit. Don't walk between the fire and an Indian, walk only behind them."

"Anything else?" she asked impatiently.

"Yes. Don't sit cross-legged like the men. Sit on

your heels or with your legs to the side. And don't speak unless directly spoken to."

"Terrific."

Once they were both inside the tipi, Jodi did as she was told, veering off to the left and waiting. Cord stepped to the right, hunching his shoulders slightly so he didn't look as tall as he was. He knew that Indians were sometimes sensitive about their shorter stature.

The eight elderly men gathered around the fire did not look up to acknowledge Diamondback's presence. Nor did they appear to notice the woman. Instead they stared quietly into the fire as if finding some inspiration in its steady flames.

Cord recognized each of the men. They were famous among Indians and whites alike. Among the Indians for bravery, among the whites for ruthlessness. They looked older than their ages, thinner than the times Cord had battled them as a captain in the U.S. cavalry. But that was under a different name, his fourth. Before his past had caught up with him again.

The oldest of the group sat cross-legged in the middle. This was Stone Axe, one of the leaders at Little Big Horn. He was wearing a collarless white cotton shirt and a leather vest. A thin braid of black hair hung down the left side of his head and a single grey feather drooped down the right side.

"Sit," he said softly.

Cord stepped up to the ring of men and took his place opposite Stone Axe. He nodded at Jodi who eased back into the shadows and sat with her legs out to one side, though she made a rebellious face as she did so. Cord kept himself from smiling.

"You know of our ways," Stone Axe acknowledged, obviously pleased.

"I have been privileged with some such knowledge."

Stone Axe switched from English to a Teton dialect. "Do you speak our language as well?"

"Some, though not as well as you speak mine," Cord responded in Teton.

Stone Axe nodded to the other elderly warriors, who each muttered approval.

"We will speak your language then," Stone Axe said in English. "I learned it as a youth so that we could trade our horses with the whites. But they used it to cheat us. I learned more language so that we might make treaty with the whites. But they cheated us again. Now I learn it to make war. In war there can be no cheating."

Cord said nothing, his eyes locked with Stone Axe's old eyes.

"You have fought Indians," Stone Axe said. It wasn't a question.

"Yes."

"As a soldier?"

"Yes."

"Where?"

"Red River War. I was at the battle of Palo Duro Canyon."

Stone Axe nodded gravely. "Commanche and Kiowa tribes. Satanta, Big Tree, Tsatangya. All brave warriors."

"All shipped to prison in Florida by General Sherman."

"Yes. Florida." He stared into the fire for a long minute, as if he could actually see Florida in there. Finally he addressed Cord again. "Why did you shoot this man who stole our horse?"

"He was following my woman and me."

"Why?"

Cord shrugged. "I don't know. Your bullet stopped his lying tongue forever."

"Yes. I shot him myself." He smiled, pointing at the rifle leaning against the tipi pole. "Winchester."

The warrior next to Stone Axe studied Cord suspiciously. "What is your name?"

Cord recognized him as Kicking Fox, Stone Axe's younger brother. "I am called Diamondback."

"I have heard this name before," Kicking Fox said. "It is not a white name."

"No, it is a gift from the Shoshoni tribe."

"Yes," Stone Axe nodded vigorously. "Yes, I know of this name."

Kicking Fox was still suspicious. "Can you prove you are the person called Diamondback?"

Cord looked over his shoulder at Jodi. Her face was hidden in the dark corner, but she could see him clearly. He was trapped. They wanted proof of his identity and there was only one kind of proof he could offer.

He started unbuttoning his shirt. There was no other way to save their lives but to be honest with these people. Anything less would result in his and Jodi's death. But in proving who he was to them, he would be revealing who he really was to Jodi. And that could prove even more dangerous later.

But he had no choice.

The last button slid free and Cord pulled his shirt over his massive shoulders. His scarred skin gleamed fiercely in the flickering light of the fire.

"Oh my God!" Jodi cried, bolting to her feet with a scream. "It can't be. *It can't be!*"

11.

"Assassin!" she hissed, her mouth snarling with hate. Even with her face cowled by heavy shadows, the fire glinted off her bared teeth and moist eyes like a coyote trapped at the back of cave. She pointed an accusing finger at Cord as if she hoped to pierce his heart with it. "You're real name is Christopher Deacon. *Murderer!*"

"Silence!" Stone Axe said angrily. "You have not been spoken to." He shook his head with disgust as he questioned Cord. "Will white woman never be more than spoiled children?"

"Some men find this . . . charming," Cord said.

Stone Axe considered this for a moment, then nodded. "I can see this might be so. For a short time." He studied Jodi for a moment, who had wisely returned to her seated position. "Yes. It is possible."

Kicking Fox interrupted with a probing stare. "We see by your many scars that you have the same markings of the rattlesnake. But yours are not spirit-given, born with you as is the snake's."

"No," Cord said, making no effort to hide them now. He must not appear to be ashamed of them in any way, for that would suggest guilt. And in truth he was not ashamed of them. They were a reminder of what he had done. And why. In a strange way, sitting there with his shirt off, his white cross-hatched scars exposed, he felt a sense of relief. More, of power. As if they were mighty wings he'd had to hide from a jealous world. "No, they are not spirit-given. They are from battle."

"Not with Indians," Stone Axe said.

"No, with whites."

Kicking Fox mumbled something to his brother and Stone Axe nodded. Both men stared at Diamondback for a moment.

"You have abandoned your white name and kept the one bestowed upon you by Indians. In doing this, you have opened yourself to being treated as an Indian by other whites. To do so is not the white way."

"Indian children are named soon after birth by the medicine man or child's father," Cord said. "But once he becomes a man he may change his name if he so wishes to one recalling a dream, a vision, a brave deed. The Shoshoni honored me with this name for a deed I performed for them. Although I did a similar deed for the whites, most did not understand, and they have chosen to disgrace my name instead. Many hate me because of the lies about my deed. This woman is like that. So I keep my Indian name because, like you, whites would not suspect that anyone would chose such a name over a white name."

Stone Axe nodded, as did Kicking Fox and the other elders. "This tastes like truth. We know of how whites use lies against their enemies." He reached behind him and picked up a long carved pipe. With the point of his knife he began cleaning it. Suddenly everyone stood up.

Cord stood up and turned to Jodi. "Once he starts cleaning his pipe that means we're supposed to leave."

She rose to her feet, glaring into his eyes, her face clenched like a fist. When he reached to guide her out of the tipi, she shrugged roughly out of his grasp and marched out ahead of him.

The young warrior who had escorted them to Stone Axe's tipi earlier was waiting outside, Cord's .45 still tucked comfortably in his waistband. He scowled at Cord and gestured for them to follow him. But Kicking Fox stopped them after a few steps.

"Diamondback," he called, catching up. His eyes were lighter than Stone Axe's, and much shrewder. Stone Axe had spent all his trust in whites over the years, but Kicking Fox had never had any. He stood a head shorter than Cord, but he squared his shoulders as if he were looking down at the taller man. "First we perform the Ghost Dance, then my brother will give you his decision. My son, Feathered Wing, will return you to the lodge to wait."

"Thank you," Cord said.

Kicking Fox grunted and stomped off in the opposite direction.

So, the young brave was Kicking Fox's son, Stone Axe's nephew. Harming him in an effort to escape would only make their dilemma worse. Cord slipped his shirt back on as they walked.

They were lead to a different tipi than before, for which Cord was grateful. Things were going to be difficult enough now without Red Cummings' corpse lying around to further spook Jodi.

Feathered Wing pointed at the door flap and Jodi ducked in, ignoring the protocol Cord had taught her earlier. Feathered Wing grinned smugly at Cord for not being able to control his woman. Cord lowered his head and entered the tipi, feeling the buffalo hide flap thrown down behind him, slapping his butt.

There was a waning fire in the center, not enough to throw off any serious light. Not enough light for him to see where Jodi was. Or what it was in her hand. Or how to defend himself when she suddenly clubbed him on the back of the head.

12.

He stumbled forward like a bludgeoned steer, his fractured cheek thudding into the dirt. Immediately he rolled away from her attack, but before he could twist around to defend himself, she clubbed him across the back.

"What the hell—" he hollered.

Another blow cracked against his arm. A tender knob swelled near his elbow.

From that last blow, he now had a rough idea where she was. He quickly kicked out a wide sweep of his booted foot until it collided with something soft and fleshy.

"Oommff," she wheezed, falling backwards into the side of the tent.

Cord scrambled to his feet and hurried toward her, but before he'd taken three steps she was on him again, her claws gouging for his eyes, her teeth clamped onto his neck. Her legs scissored around his thighs, riding his hip, which caused him to struggle just to keep his balance. Low growling sounds vibrated from the back of her throat.

"Damn!" he shouted, fending off the slashing fingernails with one hand while trying to pry loose her gnashing teeth from his neck with the other. Just when he thought he had her under control, she unclenched her legs and slammed a free knee into his crotch. He doubled over slightly and she used the opportunity to sink her teeth back into his raw neck.

"Enough, damn it!" he bellowed, grabbing her hair roughly and twisting it tightly around his hand in a wrenching knot, forcing her head backwards. She strained against his power, her mouth open, her teeth glistening with saliva and fresh blood. With a sudden flash, she swept her claws across his cheek like a cougar, plowing out several deep inches of skin. His face stung from the attack. "I said *enough*," he snarled and snapped his knee into *her* crotch.

"Ooowwww!" she yelled, dropping to her knees and grasping both hands between her legs.

"Hurts, huh?" Cord said.

She writhed on the ground trying to catch her breath, tears of pain spilling from both eyes. Finally she sucked in enough air to gasp, "You bastard."

Diamondback found the gnarled hunk of firewood she'd clubbed him with and threw it on the few weak embers of the dying fire. He gathered some kindling scraps, scattered them lightly near the embers, and blew. The orange embers suddenly glowed a fierce red, igniting the kindling and finally the log. By the time Jodi pulled herself to a hunched sitting position, the fire was bright and lively. Cord sat on the opposite side, occasionally tossing in wood as he watched her.

"Is it all out of your system?" he asked.

"Not by a long shot." Her voice was hoarse and weak. One hand still unembarrassedly massaged her tender crotch. "I'll see you pay. Once we get out of here I'll tell the whole world who you are and what name you've been hiding under."

"You're assuming a lot, not the least of which is that we'll get out of here."

"Oh, we'll get out. After all that horseshit you flung at them Indians about brave deeds and such, they'll let you go."

"You underestimate them, Jodi. My name comes from the Shoshoni, and the Sioux aren't overly fond of them lately since they're both competing for the same meager pickings of buffalo."

"Still, it's an Indian name."

"Yes, the result of me settling a dispute between some ranchers and the Shoshonis near Fort Hall."

"You a judge. That's a laugh." She spat into the fire. "When a real judge gets a hold of you, you'll find out what justice is."

Cord listened to the drums and chanting outside as the Sioux began their Ghost Dance. It was a slow beat that subtly but steadily increased pace until his own heart seemed to beat faster as it tried to keep up with the heavy drums. He stared through the fire at Jodi, her light reddish hair even more intense as they reflected the leaping flames. Her eyes sparkled with fear and hate and disappointment.

He had not told his story to anyone in years. What was the point? No one would believe him, not in the face of the rumors they'd heard, the lies they'd read. Not when confronted with the list of charges against him: Murder, Piracy, Treason. And others. No, once they heard his real name—Christopher Deacon—their minds were made up. Their hands would be reaching for a gun before they'd even heard the rest.

He grit his teeth at the terrible irony that haunted his life. He had achieved a dual fame. Under his adopted name of Cord Diamondback he had carved a reputation as a tough but fair judge. It was a name some feared, but all respected. Yet under his true name, Christopher Deacon, he had earned only hatred. Like the hatred that burned in Jodi's eyes right now.

"You killed him," she said. "You assassinated him."

"Yes."

She seemed surprised that he admitted it. "Don't you know what you've done? He would have been President someday. Everybody said so. Senator Fallows was the most popular man in the West, loved by everyone. Even in Washington he was respected and honored. I even danced with him once at the White House. A goddamn waltz. In honor of the French ambassador's new bride." She brushed away a stray tear. "He asked me all about my family and plans. Promised to help me if I ever needed. And you had to kill him. A nobody, a nothing like you. . . ." A sob caught in her throat. "You're no better than John Wilkes Booth. Worse, I think, for the horrible way you killed him. Butcher!"

Cord watched her with a quiet patience, his face a rigid mask. Her loathing was so intense it needed to spend itself. The death of Senator Billy Fallows had the same effect even on those who hated politics and politicians. To almost everyone the Senator had become a symbol of the best virtues of the young West: toughness, fairness, neighborliness. Those who were never sure exactly what he did in office, had heard enough good said about him to like him. He had been fairly young and handsome with a colorful past that included fighting Indians and making himself a millionaire. Like the perfect father everyone wished they'd had. His was a life that inspired others, gave them hope. And as far as most people knew, a crazy young drifter named Christopher Deacon had brutally murdered him one night at his home. Yes, that part was true, but the real truth, the complete truth was even more sinister—the kind that no one would ever believe because no one would want to believe. So Cord never bothered to tell it.

But he knew even now that tonight he was about to make an exception. Somehow as he stared at Jodi Lawrence through the bright tangled flames, he knew he must tell her. She would hate him for it, this too he knew. But it was time to try.

He studied her angry face now as if seeing it for the first time. Her thick hair was tossed and powdered with dirt from their wrestling, but the intense flames of the fire brought out dark red highlights like thin streams of smouldering lava flowing through her hair. The crescent boot heel bruise over her right eye made her look older and more mature. The hate that wrinkled her face and twisted her mouth wrung away her former prim prettiness and gave her a fresh raw beauty. Gone was the childish pout to the lips and belligerant tilt of her head. Now her beauty looked more durable, more savage. Her lips were full and wet, slightly swollen from their battle. A drop of his blood from when she'd bit him was dried and flaking just below her lower lip. Her nostrils flared as she stared back at him, as if she needed all the air she could get to stoke her rage. He could hear the air rushing in and being forced out with each breath she took. Her slivered eyes were angled like swooping hawks, and over each winged a thin hooked eyebrow. The menacing effect was heightened by the high sloping cheekbones so sharp they might be lethal.

"Stop staring at me," she snapped, spraying saliva like venom.

Cord ignored her, his eyes burrowing deeper into

hers. When he spoke his voice was deep but gentle, and though she was certain she didn't want to hear what he was about to say, she felt compelled to lean closer to him.

"I was sixteen when I ran away from home. Not that I was running away from cruel parents or a tragic home life. I had the best possible family a boy could hope for. My father was the best lawyer in New Jersey and my mother was the smartest school teacher. My older brother Eric was just like my father, disciplined, studious, kind, and much too trusting for his own good. They were all good people.

"And we had some money, too. Not wealth really, but we were more than comfortable. Comfortable. I guess that's the word that annoyed me so much. I had the feeling that I was just part of a well-crafted clock, sweeping into my predetermined role. My brother was already attending Harvard Law School, just as Father had, and his father had. And I was expected to do the same. It had all been decided before I was born." He smiled at the memory. "They didn't insist or anything, I mean there were no threats. But it was understood by Eric and me that we would crush my father's heart if we didn't go. Somehow that burden was even worse than threats.

"By the time I was sixteen, arrangements were already being made that I would be in Harvard the next year. I don't know exactly what came over me that last summer as I waited for the fall semester to start, but suddenly I found myself packed and on the road to New Bedford. Less than a month later I was swabbing decks and scrubbing galleys aboard *The Quapaw*, one of the finest whaling ships ever to leave New Bedford. It was a two-year voyage that had us chasing humpbacks from the Azores to the Cape of

Good Hope to the East China Sea. By the end of those two years I was in the front of a bucking whaleboat riding the whirlpool of a monster sperm whale, stabbing my harpoon into his flanks again and again until the whole crew was drenched in a cloud-burst of blood." He pointed to his left leg. "This knee is still scarred from where it chafed against the boat's knee brace, and my hands . . ." He opened his palms to her. ". . . are still leathered with cal-louses from tugging the whale line through the chock. It was a time of learning."

"What did you learn?" Jodi asked sarcastically.

He laughed. "I learned I didn't much like whaling. Not as a lifetime career anyway. I decided to go home." Cord paused, his eyes glazing, his face sullen. "But by the time I returned to New Jersey, I had no home to go back to. My brother was ten years older than I, and even with him my parents had started having children late in life. I was a middle-aged surprise to both, though they seemed to prize me all the more for it. Still, to me my parents had always been older than those of other kids. And when I arrived back in New Jersey, I realized how much older they really had been. Mother had died almost eight months earlier of tuberculosis. She was sixty-three. Father died three months later of . . . loneliness, I guess."

"I'm sorry," Jodi said, her voice hard despite the words.

Cord shrugged. "Anyway, Eric had already gone to San Francisco to open his own law practice. That came as a bit of a shock to me, since it had always been assumed he would join Father's practice. Later, he told me that he'd envied my running off to go whaling, and that's what gave him the strength to strike off on his own. I didn't know the bastard had it in him. Well, when I wired him from New Jersey, he wired me back to go see Father's law partner, that 'arrangements' concerning me had already been made. I did, and it turned out Eric had established a fund for me to continue my education. Hell, I was just turning nineteen and the only thing I knew for certain was that I didn't want to go whaling for the rest of my life. So I attended Harvard, graduated, and somehow he persuaded me to enroll in the Law School. He was good at persuading, all very logical and reasonable." He nodded at the fire as if speaking to someone other than Jodi.

"But after my first year, I was anxious to run again, if not to whaling than to the West. I dropped out of school and travelled all the way to San Francisco, prepared to give Eric the biggest surprise of his life. But when I walked into his law office, he merely looked up from his desk, shook his head, and said, 'Well, you lasted longer than I'd thought you would.' The big ox had been expecting me for the past two years!" Cord laughed deeply, and Jodi found herself struggling not to smile. Until she sternly reminded herself of who she was smiling at. What he'd done.

"He swore he wasn't going to lecture me or try to influence my decision, but two weeks later I somehow found myself with a ship ticket for New York and a commitment to stick out law school for one more year. That was his way."

Suddenly Cord's face began to tighten, the jaw setting firmly, the teeth clenching, grinding against each other. His eyes narrowed, drifting from Jodi's face to the fire. For the first time she noticed beads of sweat glistening on his forehead. Despite the warmth of the tipi, she felt a deep chill wrapping around her neck and moved closer to the fire.

"Eric was a hell of a lawyer, but he'd never gotten over being too trusting. He was handling a rather complicated case at that time, defending someone accused of smuggling opium. He'd discovered his client was being framed to cover for someone else, and that there was much more than opium involved. White slavery. Extortion. Piracy." Diamondback shook his head grimly. "Eric thought he could go charging in and uncover the whole mess. Save the day for law and order. He barged through San Francisco in some of the sleaziest neighborhoods, turning over slimey rocks to see what would crawl out." He lifted his weary eyes and looked at Jodi. Her breathing was faster now, in shallow pants, as if she knew what he was about to say. "And under one of those rocks was the head of the whole operation. Senator Billy Fallows."

"No!" she cried. "You lie. You're lying to excuse yourself."

" 'Follow the money,' " Eric had always told me. 'That's where the truth is.' And he followed it to Senator Fallows. I was with him that night, just two days before my ship was to take me back to Harvard and a life of law and stuffy courtroom justice. We met for dinner after he'd finished interviewing a witness for the trial. After we'd eaten, we were walking down a harbor alley when we were jumped by four men. Two of them grabbed Eric and started clubbing him with blackjacks. I leaped at them, swinging wildly, trying to fight my way through to Eric. But there were too many of them. I had my hands around two of their necks, when the first cut sliced through my shirt and slashed my back from shoulder to hip. Then another. And another. Someone behind me was hacking at me with a knife. I remember the feel of that blade as it cut into my flesh, both icy cold and flaming hot at the same time. Still I wouldn't let go of the two who'd knocked Eric unconscious. But finally they wrestled me to the ground, stripped my shirt off my back, and slashed me to the bone again and again.

"Fortunately for me their anger had gotten the better of their judgment. Instead of finishing me off they left me for dead and dragged Eric away. It was supposed to look like a shanghai kidnapping, but I knew who was behind it. I had been around ships enough to know how to scrape up information. The next day I visited every waterfront bar and docked ship until I was reasonably certain where they'd taken Eric."

"But your wounds," Jodi said, her voice softer now, urgent.

Cord's lips tightened into something less than a smile. "Hate dulled my pain, as hate can sometimes do." His gaze held hers as if with hooks, until she looked away with embarrassment. "Well, by the time I found the ship it had already sailed for Mexico. It took me the rest of the day and most of my brother's money to hire a crew of vagabond sailors who didn't care how they earned their money. We stole a navy frigate at night and chased my brother's ship for two days. We captured her after a bloody battle, but Eric had already been killed and dumped overboard. It took a lot of broken bones, burned and carved flesh, but eventually I found which man had killed Eric." His eyes widened at the memory. "I hacked his head off and nailed it upside down to the foremast."

Jodi's face twisted sourly.

"But it wasn't enough. I'd killed the man who'd sunk the knife into Eric, but the man who'd ordered it was still alive. Senator William Kenneth Fallows."

"I can't believe . . ." Jodi mumbled, her voice limp and without conviction.

"It took several days for me to sneak back into San Francisco. The survivors of the ship we'd captured had made it back by then and I was wanted for piracy and murder. It took some doing, but within the week I managed to break into the Senator's home and hid in his bedroom. I waited there for three days without eating or moving, waiting for him to come home. The papers had announced his expected return on 'business,' so I knew he'd show up sooner or later.

"On that third night he came into the bedroom with a woman, the young wife of the mayor of San Francisco. I waited until they were naked and in bed before bursting in on them. She squeeled and cried, but it wasn't her I wanted. I let her go knowing that by the time she summoned help it would all be over.

"The Senator must have known it too. He begged for mercy, his fat sluggish body crumpled at my feet. I remember looking down at him and feeling almost sympathy. For a moment I thought I couldn't do it. Despite everything, all the evidence Eric had shown me, I hesitated to believe this man could be responsible." Cord seemed to stop breathing for a moment, then heaved a great sigh. "You see, I too had admired him while at Harvard. He seemed like the one honest man in a dangerously corrupt government. Looking down at him quivering and sobbing made *me* feel ashamed. After all I'd gone through, I decided at that moment to leave. I'd had enough." Cord's fist suddenly slammed onto the unburned edge of flaming log. Sparks exploded into the air, glowed brightly, then floated to the ground as dead ashes. "If he'd only kept his mouth shut! But no, he begged me to spare him, pleaded that he hadn't meant for Eric to die. That he'd only wanted him out of the way until the trial was over. That the men he'd hired from the ship had become over-zealous. He goddamn admitted the whole thing!"

"And you killed him," Jodi whispered.

Cord's eyes blazed. "Yes, I killed him. I killed him just as the papers reported. With a whaler's harpoon the way I used to kill giant whales. With a single thrust, I shoved the barbed spearhead through his bloated stomach and out his back until there was no more shaft. I watched his greasy blood gush out as he spent the last worthless minutes of his life trying to pull the barbs free."

"My God!"

"I was God!" he said quietly.

"What happened then?"

"You know most of the rest. I became the most hunted criminal in the West. Easy to spot, just look for the cross-hatch knife scars on the back. Like a diamondback rattlesnake. And I've been on the run every since."

"That's a long run."

"I changed my name and joined the cavalry for a few years. That's where I learned to shoot and ride. And box."

"Why'd you leave?"

"My colonel finally figured it out. I wasn't as clever then at covering my tracks as I am now. But by then I'd won some commendations for fighting and he couldn't believe that I could have done what everyone claimed. He confronted me and I told him the same story I just told you. He believed me, gave me a horse and a two-hour headstart."

"How'd you get into judging?"

He tossed another log onto the fire. "Tradition. I owe my family something. They believed in justice, so do I. My brother died for it, I killed for it. It's that simple."

Jodi shook her head. "Nothing about you is simple."

"Do you believe me?" He was surprised at how much he cared about her answer.

"I-I don't know yet. I have to sort it all out."

"Fair enough."

They sat on opposite sides of the fire without speaking for almost an hour. Occasionally Cord would drop another log on the flames, but other than that there was no movement. Outside the tipi the drums still beat, the Indians still chanted and danced.

Then it stopped.

The sudden quiet was ominous. Cord nodded with assurance at Jodi, who scooted even closer to the fire, hugging herself tightly.

The door flap was wisked open and Feathered Wing waved for them to come out.

"What now?" Jodi asked.

"Now we find out what they're going to do with us."

As they were lead back to Stone Axe's tipi, they saw most of the tribe still milling around where they'd just completed their ceremony. They were staring knowingly at Jodi and Diamondback.

"Why are they looking at us that way?" Jodi asked.

"I don't know. Maybe nothing more than a reaction to the Ghost Dance."

"The what?"

"Ghost Dance. Some Paiute started the whole thing

about ten years ago, though it's only caught on with a few tribes, mostly in Nevada, California, and Oregon. They believe that all white people are going to fall into huge holes in the ground and be swallowed up, while all the dead Indians will return to replace them and enjoy all the things left behind by the whites."

"That's kind of creepy."

He shrugged. "It's kind of sad."

She turned to look at him as they walked. There it was again, he noticed, that gentleness and vulnerability. Only this time she didn't try to squeeze it off. She smiled bravely, though he could tell she was scared. "Where do you learn all that stuff?"

"Folklore interests me."

Feathered Wing halted in front of Stone Axe's tipi and grunted for them to enter. Jodi stepped aside to allow Cord to duck through first. She followed close behind, veering to the left just as she'd done before.

Cord nodded approval to her, and she tried to smile again, but she couldn't. He noticed her lips were quivering now.

"Diamondback!" Stone Axe called cheerily. "Come in."

Cord crossed his long legs and sat across the fire in his former place. He moved slowly, taking enough time to study the faces of the elders. All stared impassively into the fire. Except Kicking Fox. There was a sly twinkling in his hooded eyes that disturbed Cord.

"We have decided," Stone Axe said, his smile huge with satisfaction. Another bad sign. "The Ghost Dance has given me new hope, made me more charitable toward my enemy."

Cord listened without expression, his face as stony as the elders.

"We have agreed to honor your Shoshoni name and deed and allow you to leave with your horse and gun and hair."

"Thank you for your generosity," Cord nodded. "We will leave immediately." He started to rise.

"No!" Stone Axe said, his smile stretched over round worn teeth. "I said *you* may leave, Diamondback. But the red-haired woman stays with us."

13.

Diamondback rose to his feet, and smiled. "Well, that's it then. Thanks for your hospitality. I'll be riding out now."

"*Cord!*" Jodi screamed, leaping to her feet with terror.

"Sit, woman!" Kicking Fox commanded.

Stone Axe chuckled. "Perhaps you are right, Diamondback. Her manners can be charming. We shall see."

Cord laughed. "I'm sure you'll be pleased. Now, if I can just get my gear, I'd like to make it back to Walkers Rest."

"Diamondback, you pig!" she yelled so violently the words scraped her voice hoarse. Tears streamed down her face. "I believed you, you bastard! I believed your whole damn story."

Cord ignored her, as did the Indians. Despite her shrieking outbursts, they quietly continued their conversation as if they were alone.

"I'll need my guns," Cord said.

Kicking Fox smiled thinly. "Feathered Wing will ride with you for a while and give them to you when you are far from here."

"Fine. Thanks again." He started for the door flap.

"Vic will get me out of this," Jodi hissed at him.

"And when he does I'll make sure he catches you and cuts your balls off."

Cord brushed the flap open and started to duck through. He hesitated a moment, then turned around to face the elders. "You know, I don't want to be any trouble or anything, but it's getting awfully dark. Since you already have a fire going, do you mind if I stay here until after I've eaten? Won't take me long."

Stone Axe waved with a generous smile. "Stay, Diamondback. Eat as our guest. You are welcome."

The elders nodded approval of Stone Axe's grand gesture of hospitality. Except Kicking Fox. He narrowed his eyes and rubbed his chin suspiciously.

"Thanks," Cord smiled. "And maybe later we can play some cards.

Stone Axe pushed his bow toward Cord. It was a magnificent weapon made from ash and strung with two buffalo sinews twisted together. He'd already pushed in the buckskin case with attached quiver and arrows.

"How many?" he asked Cord with a frown.

Cord knitted his eyebrows. "Two . . . make that one. I'll take a chance." He tossed in one card.

Stone Axe carefully peeled off a single card and handed it to Cord. Since his tribe had been on the run, they'd been unable to buy cards, so they'd made their own from dried buffalo hides. The designs were copied from an old Spanish deck they'd won from some Mexican cowboys.

Stone Axe threw away three of his own and counted out three new ones. As he added each to his hand he looked pleased.

"I break you now, Diamondback." He snapped his fingers and pointed at his Winchester against the tipi.

An elder brought it to him. Stone Axe smiled as he laid it next to his bow.

Cord studied his cards with an uncertain frown, looking at the goods in the pot, then frowning even harder at his hand. He sighed deeply, shook his head, folded the hand, and started to toss them in. Then he stopped. "Damn it, Stone Axe, I think you're bluffing. You can't have much." He nodded to Feathered Wing, who handed him his Winchester. He pushed that into the pot. His Smith & Wessson Shofield .45 was already in. "And I'll raise you . . ." He looked around the tipi. ". . . hell, I'll raise you my horse. A damn fine appaloosa."

"Yes," Stone Axe said eagerly, brushing away Kicking Fox's cautionary hand. "I wager my horse too. What are your cards? I have two pair. Two aces, two kings."

Cord frowned even more. "I'm afraid all I have are fours," he said as he slowly flipped over each card, one at a time. A ten. An eight. A four of cudgels. A four of coins. He hesitated, flipped it over. A four of swords. He shrugged. "But I have three of them. Guess I win."

A low grumble worked its way around the circle of elders like a distant thunder. Stone Axe looked disgusted with himself and angry at Cord.

"Another hand!" he demanded.

"Enough for tonight," Kicking Fox advised.

But Stone Axe wanted more. Indians had been voracious gamblers for centuries before whites had ever set foot on this land. They gambled among themselves, between tribes, and with whites. Sioux women gambled their pots and shawls away on a toss of painted plum stones. Entire tribes were known to wager all their possessions on a single foot race. Cord knew all that, counted on it, if he was going to get Jodi safely out of here.

"Well, Stone Axe," Cord said, "I'd be pleased to play another hand with you, but I already own your gun, your bow, and your horse. What else have you got to offer?"

"Another horse. We have more horses."

Cord shook his head. "Two horses are about all I can handle right now. And so are two Winchesters. Naw, I don't see where you've got anything I need." He started to rise.

"No, wait," Stone Axe said.

Cord watched him as he looked around the tipi. The chief was thinking feverishly, the way losing gamblers often do. His eyes were narrow and scheming when they finally stopped on Jodi, who sat quietly exhausted against the far skirt of the tipi. She had yelled and screamed until her voice had given out completely. Now she sat in a collapsed heap, resigned to her doom.

"The red-haired woman," Stone Axe said. "We play for her."

Cord screwed up his face. "I don't know." He scratched chin and shook his head. "Nope. She's not worth all this stuff I won." He started to rise again. "Thanks again."

"Two women, Diamondback," Stone Axe said, holding up two fingers. "I throw in another woman." He saw Cord hesitate. "And another horse. One more hand."

Diamondback sighed, drooped his gear to the ground, and sat down. "My turn to deal."

He dealt the clumsy buffalo hide cards and waited for Stone Axe to make up his mind on how many cards he wanted to draw.

"Three cards," Stone Axe said.

Cord tossed him three cards, then gave himself three cards. "No point in bluffing around now. Our bet's already been made. The cards talk."

Both men turned over their cards.

"You bastard!"

No reply.

"You son of a bitch!"

No reply.

"You goddamn shitheel!" Jodi flung her arms around Cord's neck and hugged him tightly. Her voice was dry and scratchy from yelling earlier. "Why didn't you at least give me a hint or a sign or *something* to let me know you weren't going to just leave me there?"

"Because if I'd have signaled you they probably would have picked up on it. Besides, you made them believe that you hated me."

"I did hate you." She looked embarrassed.

"Well, you're free now. All we have to do is ride out in the morning. We still have work up in the mountains."

"I don't see why we can't leave now. The sooner we get away from here the better I'll feel."

"Because it would be insulting to leave now, right after we cleaned Stone Axe out. We have to accept his hospitality."

She flopped down near the fire and sighed with relief. "I know you were doing the best you could, Cord, but still, what would've happened if you'd have lost?"

"I couldn't have lost."

"What do you mean?"

"I cheated."

"You what?" Her eyes widened. "I mean, what if they would have caught you?"

He sat near the fire and pulled off his boots. "Well, then they would have killed me. But don't worry, Stone Axe was too busy trying to cheat me to pay much attention to what I was doing."

"I didn't think Indians cheated."

He laughed. "They're just people like everybody else. The Shoshones once bought all the decks of cards at a particular store, took them home and marked the decks, then pled poverty and sold them back to the store at a quarter of what they'd paid for them. Now they knew that the Piutes bought all their cards at this same store. So they began gambling very heavily with the Piutes, eventually cleaning them out of just about everything they owned."

Jodi laughed, as much from the release of built up tension as from the story. "Well, we're safe at last."

Suddenly the door flap snapped open and Feathered Wing ducked into the tipi. His eyes were wide with anger. He glared at Cord with such intense unmistakable hate that Jodi feared he would lunge at Cord's throat. Following behind him entered a young Sioux woman about Jodi's age, but several inches taller. She nodded politely at Cord and moved to the right of the entrance, her head bowed.

Feathered Wing spun wordlessly to leave, paused to exchange glances with the young woman, and burst out of the tipi. Cord recognized in their exchange a romantic relationship.

"What do you want?" Jodi asked her.

The young woman ignored Jodi and addressed Cord. "I am called River Pony. Stone Axe has sent me to be yours." She spoke without bitterness or anger, only a vague sense of loss.

"Cord, I don't understand," Jodi said. "You mean he's really going to give you this woman? Just like that?"

"I won her."

"Yes, but you chea—" Jodi stopped herself. "What now?"

"Now we go to sleep and worry about it in the morning. I'm still aching from my fight yesterday."

Jodi and Cord began gathering hides and blankets into their separate beds. River Pony immediately rushed forward and nudged Cord out of the way.

"I do," she said, arranging hides and blankets into a cozy nest.

"Oh, brother," Jodi snorted sarcastically as she climbed, fully dressed except for her boots, into her bed. With her head propped on her hand, she watched with a combination of anger and amusement.

When his bed was finally made, River Pony began tugging at Cord's clothing. "Very warm in there," she explained, nodding at the bed.

Cord knew from experience just how warm it was in there, and allowed her to help him off with his shirt. "I'll do the rest," he said, stripping off his denim pants, but leaving on his underwear. He climbed between the hides and blankets. "Where are you going to sleep?" he asked River Pony.

She looked confused for a moment, then quickly pulled her buckskin dress over her head. She was naked underneath. "With you, Diamondback."

Jodi sat straight up. "What?"

The dying fire cast an orange glow inside the tipi. It made River Pony's dark skin look soft and moist. Her oaken nipples poked pertly out as she sat on her heels, patiently waiting for a decision to be made.

"She can't sleep with you while I'm in here," Jodi protested. "That's perverted! Sick!"

Cord sat up. "Look, River Pony. I know you are doing what is expected of you. But I can also see that you have feelings for Feathered Wing. I promise you that when we leave in the morning you will stay behind to be with him."

River Pony smiled. "You are kind, Diamondback, but you do not understand. I was once wed, but my man was killed in battle. Feathered Wing would have been mine, but Stone Axe has given his word to you. This person is yours now."

"But I will arrange so that you may stay here. Stone Axe will not be dishonored."

River Pony thought about that for a minute before speaking. "We shall see what will be when it is. Tomorrow is tomorrow. Now is now." She flipped back the covers and slid her naked body next to Cord.

"For God's sake, Diamondback," Jodi said, "you aren't going to . . . do anything."

"This person is yours now," River Pony said, wrapping her naked leg around Cord. "You can not give me back without first taking me. They would think you were giving me back because I was not worthy. Feathered Wing would not want me then. You must."

"Can't you just pretend?" Jodi asked.

"Pretend?"

"Make believe he took you."

She frowned. "He would know. The lie would be worse than the deed."

"Jesus, Cord," Jodi said aghast. "You aren't really going to?"

Cord sighed deeply and shrugged. "Doesn't look like I have much choice. We want to leave her behind in the morning, and she won't stay unless she can keep her honor. This is the only way."

"Well, what the hell am I supposed to do while you two are, uh, going at it? Leave?"

"No, they won't let you out of the tipi. I suggest you turn your back and stop up your ears. Indians can sometimes be a little noisy."

Jodi huffed angrily, twisting her face toward the side of the tipi, her back to Cord and River Pony. Immediately she could hear the rustling as River Pony tugged Cord's underwear off. She pulled the covers over her head.

But the noises still came!

With the covers keeping her hidden, she flipped back around and peaked out with one eye through a little flap she made. Perhaps it was nasty to spy, but she felt compelled. Her heart thudded in her ears as she watched.

Cord and River Pony were both on their knees, arms wrapped around each other, kissing with a passion that Jodi thought was more than just duty. Jodi felt the stirrings of anger that she couldn't account for.

They were speaking Teton now, thank God. At least she wouldn't have to endure any romantic drivel.

River Pony was beautiful, Jodi had to admit. They were the same age, yet the Indian's body seemed so much firmer, hardier than hers. In the dim firelight her dark skin seemed smoother, silkier, like a warm pond. Her breasts were a little smaller than Jodi's, but they thrust out with firm insistence, the long nipples hard and brown as bark. Jodi watched Cord reach out and gently cup one of the breasts in his huge hand. The contrast of his mottled bruises and rough skin next to her pure smoothness struck Jodi as strangely exciting. River Pony laid one hand over his and crushed them both tighter to her breast, swooning slightly from the sensation.

River Pony's back arched and mouth opened, and Jodi felt a sudden shiver of delight rattle along her own spine. A damp tingling spread across her abdomen and lower. My God, she thought with shock, turning her head away again.

Cord heard the rustling behind him and knew that Jodi was watching them. He didn't like that idea much, but there didn't seem to be a lot he could do about it right now. River Pony had insisted that having sex was the only way to maintain her honor, so he would oblige her. Still, he didn't care much for having an audience, even if River Pony didn't mind. What made matters even worse was her stipulation that he take her from behind because she was saving the face-to-face position for Feathered Wing. Not that he minded that way, it just made having an audience all the more a nuisance. After all, since he was going to do it any way, he would like to enjoy it. Something that would be hard to do with Jodi spying on their every move.

Jodi kept her back to the proceedings for a full minute before writhing back around and reopening her tiny flap. What she saw made her take a deep breath.

River Pony was on her hands and knees facing Cord, who was only on his knees. She lowered her head until it was level with his throbbing erection, then using her hand pressed it flat against his hard stomach so that it pointed straight up. It looked strangely vulnerable nestled among the sharp ridges of his tight stomach muscles. River Pony lowered her head even further, poking her tongue out as far as it would go. Slowly, almost teasingly, she cupped his drooping balls with her pink tongue, running it up the entire length of his penis. She did it several times, each time slower than the last.

Jodi opened her secret flap wider. Now River Pony was holding each ball in her mouth, working it around with her tongue like candy. Cord's head tilted backwards, hands on his hips, his mouth slack with pleasure. At the tip of his penis a pearl of semen sparkled in the firelight. River Pony noticed, smiled, then licked it up. Jodi caught herself licking her own lips at the same time. Jesus no, she scolded herself, closing the flap. But not all the way.

When River Pony pulled away, Jodi could see Cord's thick penis glistening from saliva and semen, pointing up like a tipi pole. Her mouth felt strangely dry and empty.

River Pony turned her back toward Cord now, and leaned forward until her head rested on the ground, but she was still on her knees. Her smooth full backside was completely exposed to Cord. She reached around with both hands and tugged apart each cheek of her ass, displaying pink and dripping folds of delicate flesh. Cord's penis bobbed on its own, like a race horse straining at the reins. She said something in Teton and Cord cupped his hand between her legs, stroking the shiny black pubic hairs. A slick film of moisture glistened on his palm where he touched her.

Jodi was amazed at how straight the Indian's pubic hairs were, not curly and matted like white women. As Cord's hand continued to stroke, Jodi found her own hand had drifted between her legs and was rubbing slightly. She could smell River Pony's fertile sex all the way over here, different than her own scent. Somehow richer, like a thick venison gravy.

River Pony was rocking back and forth now, in rhythm with Cord's stroking, humming a strange tune. Her eyes were closed and her hands were pulling her cheeks even further apart. Two of Cord's fingers disappeared inside River Pony's soft hole, and Jodi gasped as her own hand tightened on her crotch. This is crazy, she thought, but couldn't stop. She rubbed faster now, imitating Cord's pace.

The Indian woman giggled and said something and Cord laughed. He walked forward on his knees until he was very close to her. With one hand guiding his penis, he entered her slowly until his abdomen pressed against her ass. She moaned softly and tucked her hands under her head.

Then the movement started.

They both ground together at first in a slow rotating motion. Cord's hands rested lightly on her protruding hip bones. But soon the pace began to speed up, faster and faster, until they were no longer rotating, but merely thrusting against each other, their wet skin slapping and slushing with each movement. Cord's massive hands gripped her hips tightly now, his fingers making pale indentations on her dark skin. His broad shoulders rippled with muscles as he rammed forward, slamming into her. The white scars across his back were thick as rope, each sloping and intersecting, indeed like a diamondback rattlesnake. Somehow that image excited Jodi even more.

River Pony was throwing her hips up to meet his thrusts with such energy that she lifted completely off her knees. Her breathing was labored now, and she was screeching noises that sounded like an attacking owl. This sound mixed with Cord's increasing grunts excited Jodi even further. She rubbed faster.

Then River Pony let out a long high-pitched yell

and Cord lifted her hips off the ground, grit his teeth, and shoved his own pelvis forward. They were locked together in one glorious moment of orgasm, the fire highlighting each drop of sweat on their bodies with a tiny fire all its own. They seemed somehow suspended as each quivered against the other, squeezing every last ounce of ecstasy from this moment.

As Jodi watched, she felt her own body shiver, tense, then shiver again. A grey film washed over her eyes, and she kept herself from gasping too.

When it was over, she watched Cord and River Pony climb wearily between the covers, their arms and legs wrapped longingly around each other. She closed her eyes and drifted off to sleep.

In the silence that followed, Cord watched the last embers of the fire surrender to darkness. In this darkness he made plans for how to leave River Pony and his other winnings behind without insulting or dishonoring Stone Axe. Either could result in their deaths before they'd ridden five miles.

As he considered the problem he heard soft footsteps moving outside the tipi. He had no doubt that they belonged to Feathered Wing, and that he had been crouching outside there during the whole time he had made love with River Pony. Cord shifted uncomfortably and sleeping River Pony moaned with contentment. If he took her along, Feathered Wing would kill them. If he left her behind, Stone Axe would kill them.

Diamondback stared into the darkness. There had to be a way out.

14.

Diamondback sat astride his big appaloosa and smiled down at Stone Axe's grim face. Tied to the sleek mare that once was Stone Axe's favorite, was Stone Axe's prized Winchester and his beloved ash bow with the buckskin quiver. Atop the mare was River Pony, a placid stoic expression frozen on her face. Stone Axe gazed with particular agony at the red-headed Jodi, for he had tossed sleeplessly all night lamenting his lack of dexterity at cheating that resulted in losing her.

"I guess we'll be heading out now," Cord told him. "Thanks for everything."

Stone Axe grumbled something unintelligible and waved a dismissing hand. Next to him Kicking Fox stared with eyes as cold as a mountain creek. Behind the gathered tribe, next to the horses, sulked Feathered Wing, his lips curled back over clenched white teeth, his hand resting anxiously on the knife in his belt. Cord could see in his black eyes that before the day was over, somewhere along the trail, Feathered Wing would try to plunge that knife of his into Cord's heart. Cord wondered how many of his buddies he'd convince to join him in his revenge. Probably enough.

Cord slowly lead Jodi and River Pony toward the

edge of camp, holding back for what he knew was coming. Hoped was coming.

"Diamondback!" Stone Axe shouted.

Cord pulled up his horse and swung around to face the chief.

"One more game, Diamondback!"

"Hell, I've already got more than I want. More than I know what to do with."

"You can sell hides. We have plenty of hides."

Cord looked unconvinced. "No offense, Stone Axe, but those things smell something awful. I'd just as soon not have to ride with a noseful of them." He started to jerk the horse back toward the trail.

"Another woman?" Stone Axe offered. "We have plenty women too."

"Got more than I can handle right here."

"Horses? You pick."

Diamondback scratched his neck in consideration. "My pick, huh?"

"Yes."

He hesitated, not wanting to fall into their trap too easily. He looked over at the horses bunched together, gave an admiring whistle. "Aw, what the hell. One more game."

Stone Axe smiled happily, but it was Kicking Fox's triumphant grin that clued Cord he'd convinced them.

Cord hopped off his horse and rubbed his hands together. "One more game you said, now that's all I intend to play. So make your bet now. This is your last chance."

Stone Axe nodded at Kicking Fox. "Any horse you chose," the chief's brother explained, "plus three buffalo hides and any widow you want. In exchange, you wager all that Stone Axe has lost, plus the redhaired woman."

Cord sucked in a deep breath. He thought they'd be content to win back just what they'd lost, not get greedy and want Jodi back too. He'd have to be careful now. "No," he shook his head. "Five buffalo hides and she stays with me."

Kicking Fox frowned, his face wrinkling as he exchanged glances with Stone Axe. Stone Axe stared up into Cord's eyes, two hardened warriors probing, testing the other's limits.

"Done," Stone Axe smiled.

"Okay," Cord nodded, "let's shuffle those cards."

"No cards," Kicking Fox said. He grinned wolfishly.

"No cards," Stone Axe repeated, his smile broadening.

"What the hell do you mean? You said one more hand of cards!"

"No," Kicking Fox explained. "We said 'one more game.' Cards is not the game we choose."

Cord took off his hat and threw it angrily to the ground, kicking it once for effect. "If that isn't the lowest, cheatingest . . . Goddamn, I guess you did learn something about using our language. Okay, what game are we going to play?"

Stone Axe chuckled. The rest of the tribe chuckled along, pleased at how their chief had fooled the white man. "Throwing-them-off-their-horses."

"Damn it, Stone Axe," Cord sighed. "You tricked me."

Stone Axe nodded acknowledgment at the compliment, his smile as wide as his face would allow.

Cord stripped off his shirt and hung it over the pommel on Jodi's saddle.

"What's going on?" she whispered.

"Throwing-them-off-their-horses. It's a Sioux game that boys play. You strip naked, climb onto a bareback horse, and charge at each other, trying to wrestle the other off his horse onto the ground."

"Yeah, well, don't look now, but Feathered Wing is taking off his clothes."

Cord made a face. "I was hoping they'd pick a less painful game."

"You can take him, can't you?"

"That's the whole point. I don't want to. But I'm going to have to put up a convincing loss. And that means taking a beating."

"Like the one you took last night from River Pony," she said icily.

"I wish." He stripped off the rest of his clothing and turned to face Feathered Wing, who was already astride his horse. Some of the older Indian women pointed at Diamondback's naked body and nodded appreciatively or giggled lewdly.

The early morning sun reflected off the raised scars on his back making them look like bleached vines crawling across his skin. The sight of his huge chest, V-ing down to a tight hard waist thrilled Jodi as she watched him lift the saddle off his horse and hop on to the bareback.

The two men rode out into the neighboring field, facing each other atop their stomping mounts at a distance of a hundred yards. When they heard Stone Axe's shout, they galloped at each other, shouting encouragement at their horses. Clouds of brown dust billowed up around each as they stampeded closer and closer.

Feathered Wing leaned his chest out over the side, making an easy target for Cord to grab. But Cord had seen this trick before. He wanted to lose, but not get trampled to death in the process. He made no effort to grab at Feathered Wing's exposed torso, instead leaning over his horse's neck to make less of a target himself.

Feathered Wing realized his ruse wasn't going to work, and straightened himself, his knees pressing the sweating horse's ribs. When he was almost up to Cord, he suddenly jerked the reins and swung his horse in the same direction as Cord was going, leaping from his horse onto Cord's.

He was showing off a little for River Pony and the rest of the tribe, scornful of Diamondback because he thought the white man had been afraid to grab at him. Cord waited patiently until Feathered Wing was balanced. He didn't want to knock the anxious young man off accidentally and win. When the Indian's arm was firmly strapped around Cord's chest, trying to wrench him off the horse, Cord began to struggle. First, he slowed the horse down to a canter, at the same time trying to block the rain of stinging blows Feathered Wing was pummeling him with. Second, just to make a good showing of fighting back, he snapped his elbow backwards into Feathered Wing's stomach. Unfortunately, Feathered Wing had lurched forward at the same time, doubling the power of Cord's blow. All the air whooshed out of him as he grabbed his injured stomach and started to fall off the horse.

Cord twisted around grabbing him as he fell, pretending to wrestle with him, but actually holding him onto the horse until he caught his breath. When he felt Feathered Wing's strength increasing, he let go.

To end this battle, he needed to give the Indian lad a target. Cord pulled back his right arm as if to punch him, let his fist hang in the air for an extra second, exposing his open chin, and allowed the Feathered Wing to punch him in the jaw. He toppled off the horse, falling deliberately on his shoulders to absorb the impact.

A loud cheer rose from the Indian camp. Whooping and drum beating echoed across the field as Feathered Wing raised his arms in triumph and rode around Cord in a large taunting circle.

Cord dusted himself off and affected a limp that should convince them of his brutal defeat. By the time he'd walked back to the camp, they had his horse saddled. Stone Axe was holding his Winchester and bow, and leading his horse. Feathered Wing was holding River Pony. He grinned smugly at Cord. River Pony's face remained impassive, but there was a twinkling of thanks in her eyes as she gazed at Cord.

"Well, Stone Axe," Cord said with a disgusted shake of his head. "I guess you got the better of me this time. But watch out next time."

"Next time," Stone Axe waved, chuckling happily.

15.

Diamondback clenched his coat tighter around his throat to block out the harsh cool mountain air that was whipping around them. Leaning forward in his saddle, he peered out over the craggy ridge at the meager town of Dog Trail.

"It's so mangy it looks like it ought to be called Dog *Tail*," Jodi complained scornfully.

"It used to be," Cord said, outlining the curve of the town with a pointing finger. "Because of the way it wraps around the mountain like that. But when the miners started bringing in their families there was some strong sentiment from the wives about changing the name."

Jodi frowned skeptically. "How do you know that?"

"Names interest me."

"Hell, everything interests you. You can't possibly know everything you claim to. You must be making up half of it."

Cord shrugged and continued studying the layout of the town. The best way in, the fastest way out. Standard procedure when entering a town in which he had business.

Jodi sat silently next to him, drawing up the collar of her own coat against the chill. The sun was rolling lazily out of sight over the western slopes and every ten minutes the temperature seemed to drop another five degrees.

"What are we doing up here anyway?" she asked, shivering.

"Trying to figure a way to go in without getting shot."

"Hell, there's nothing to worry about. You're with me."

He gave her a hard look over his shoulder. "That's what I'm worried about.

"What do you mean?"

He snatched up his canteen, took a long tug of water, and smacked his lips, all the time staring at her. There was something different about her, something he couldn't quite put his finger on. "I mean that I hope you haven't forgotten our late lamented travelling companion, Virgil 'Red' Cummings."

"What about him?"

"Well, we already know he wasn't telling us the truth about where he was from. That makes me suspect that he wasn't telling us the truth about other things too."

"Like what?"

"Like maybe he wasn't working alone. Maybe somebody knew you were riding out to bring me in and didn't want either of us to come back alive."

She gazed thoughtfully down at Dog Trail, stroking the neck of her mustang as she spoke. "Doesn't make sense. Who would want me dead?"

Diamondback sighed. "You said you left a note for Curry telling him where you were going and why—"

"Not Vic!" she protested. "He loves me. He wouldn't send somebody to kill me!"

"Probably not. But just as probably everybody in town, outlaws and townspeople alike, knows by now what was in that note. They'll all be expecting us. Except for the one who sent Red."

She shook her head vigorously. "You're wrong this time. You don't know everything."

Cord swung his horse around and started back down the trail. "Guess this is a good time to find out. We'll go in the front door and see who jumps."

Jodi followed sullenly along the narrow rocky trail without saying a word. Diamondback rode ten feet in front of her, his back straight in the saddle, tensed for action, his hand hovering near his booted Winchester. He didn't like the situation at all, but it was the job he'd hired on to do so he'd follow through.

"Diamondback," Jodi called suddenly, pulling up her horse.

"Yeah?" He kept riding.

"I'm sorry, damn it."

Cord tugged his reins, swinging his appaloosa around. A puzzled expression rode his face. "Sorry? What for?"

"Nothing," she mumbled with a shrug. "Everything."

Cord nudged his horse and rode back next to her. "Run that by me again."

She stared at the pommel on her saddle with obvious embarrassment. "Aw, hell, it's just that I know I've been kind of a pain in the ass since we left the Sioux camp. After that night you and River Pony . . ." She picked idly at the latigo on her saddle. "Anyway, I know I've said some cruel things about that during the last couple days. I shouldn't have. I know you were only doing what you had to."

Cord smiled. "Well, don't make me out a saint, lady. I did manage to enjoy it somewhat."

Jodi blushed and looked away. "Well, that's your business."

Cord laughed.

"Damn you," she snapped angrily, lifting her pale blue eyes to stare at him. They seemed to shine from some internal light now, as if there was a tiny candle behind each one. "Why do you make me so damned mad sometimes?"

"Do I?"

"You know damn well you do. It's just that you confuse me so much. When I first met you I just figured you were just arrogant. But when I learned you were really Christopher Deacon, I wanted to kill you. Then after I heard your story I believed you, even sympathized with you." She shook her head. "But you're so contradictory! So unpredictable. The way you coldly, deliberately shot chunks out of Red Cummings was so brutal. How can you be the same man who needlessly risked his life just to save River Pony's honor and Stone Axe's pride? Not to mention saving my life." She sighed. "How can both those men be the same person?"

Cord took a deep breath, enjoying the tingle of cool mountain air as it rushed into his lungs. In a few minutes they'd be riding into Dog Trail, and he expected to face his toughest fight ever. And as always before a fight, he didn't feel much like talking. "Understanding me won't make any difference in how I do my job for you."

"I'm not thinking about the job right now."

"But I am." He reined his horse around and gigged him in the side.

"Bastard," she mumbled, urging her horse to follow behind. As her mustang picked his way carefully down the steep trail, she stared thoughtfully at Cord's stiff back and wondered how what was supposed to be a moment of intimate apology had gotten away from her. Her heart fluttered with anger. She was a fool to have opened herself to him. Soon she'd be back with Vic and everything would be fine, just as it had been before she'd met Diamondback.

It took them less than an hour to work their way back to the main road leading to Dog Trail. By now it was almost completely dark and Cord relaxed a bit. He felt a little less like a target now. But for added coverage, he dropped back until Jodi was flush on his left side, making him even less vulnerable from attack. If that's what they had in mind. There was no way of telling what men like these had in mind, except what they could get for themselves. Certainly they weren't going to be pleased to see him. No self-respecting outlaw would appreciate any advice on how to split their loot. But that was part of the fun, he smiled humorlessly.

As they rounded the last bend in the road, they could see the first buildings looming ahead. They approached slowly, but there was no sign of life anywhere. No lamps, no noise, no people. The only light came from the bright half moon hanging like an axe head over the town.

"Oh God, no!" Jodi gasped, jerking her horse to a halt.

Cord saw the dangling body hanging from the second story gable of the livery barn. His short fat body was naked except for the small sign around his neck and the smell of rotting flesh was powerful even at a distance. A slight breeze kept him twisting so that Cord couldn't read the sign yet. As they approached, the grizzly scene only got worse. The corpse's head was twisted at an almost comic angle.

His eyes had already been picked clean by birds. Cord noticed the healing bullet wound in the man's thigh and the hacked off ear. At first he thought the black mass around the earless hole was just crusted blood, but as they got closer, he saw it was a moving mass of hungry insects.

"J-Jesus," Jodi stuttered, shaken. "Th-That's . . ."

"That's the man who sliced off Curry's ear after Curry shot him in the leg."

She nodded, swallowing the sour taste seeping up her throat.

When they were directly under the swaying body they could finally read the sloppy hand-painted sign: WELCOME HOME, JODI!

"I'm going to be sick," Jodi warned.

Somewhere behind them, Cord heard the unmistakable sound of a rifle being levered. Followed by laughter. A crackling warbling laughter that echoed out of the dark from all directions. Cord turned slowly in his saddle and glanced around the empty street. No one. Nothing. But the laughter grew louder and louder as it seemed to get closer. He heard another rifle levered. And another. Cord stood up in his saddle and twisted around toward the barn. But when he looked up at the naked bloated corpse dangling above, he saw it suddenly lurch at him, arms and legs spread as it dove straight for him.

16.

Diamondback jerked the reins violently, rearing his horse backwards until it bumped into the flank of Jodi's mustang. Both horses skittered and snorted at the contact.

The gnarled corpse flopped harmlessly to the ground where Cord had been moments before. The crooked head smashed into a sharp rock, which split the skin but didn't bleed. The busy insects burrowing in his ragged earhole hardly seemed to notice any difference as they continued their marching about, carrying tiny chunks of flesh and brain.

"Whoa, now, easy," Cord soothed, gentling his nervous horse with soft strokes along the neck.

Jodi was having a harder time controlling her horse as he scuttled and danced sideways, stomping hooves and straining reins. "Easy, fella. Calm down, damn it."

"That ain't no way to gentle a horse," someone called from the dark. "I thought I taught you better, gal."

"Vic!" Jodi shouted at the ambling figure emerging from a dark alley between the livery barn and the barber shop.

Remembering the three rifles he'd heard levered, Cord kept his hands a fair distance from his guns.

Victor "Angel Eyes" Curry was the same age as Jodi, but there was something about the cocky way he strutted and tilted his head that made him seem even younger. The bad boy of the town that parents were always fretting about. His face was clean and smooth, though it looked like he might be trying to grow a moustache. Cord figured it would take him at least six months before anyone could be sure one way or the other. He wore a blue bandanna over his head pirate-style to cover the flap of skin that was all that was left of his right ear.

"You Diamondback?"

Cord nodded.

Curry stepped closer, a contemptuous smirk twisting his lips as he looked Cord over, deliberately inspecting him as one would a prize steer. Curry tugged absently at the knot at the back of the bandanna as he walked all the way around Cord's horse. His eyes were dark blue, with red flecks like bird tracks near the pupil. If it wasn't for the practiced mean furl of his brows, he would look like a choirboy. Cord understood the "Angel Eyes" nickname now.

"You don't look like so much to me," Curry snorted. "But then, I ain't never heard of you till Jodi here told me about you."

"Vic, aren't you glad to see me?" Jodi asked, and there was that same cautionary tone in her voice she'd used when trying to calm her spooked horse. "You haven't hardly said a word to me."

"Hell, yes, I'm glad to see you. Gave you a fancy welcoming didn't I?"

"Nearly scared me to death you mean."

"You deserved it, for riding out like that without asking me first." He leaned forward, whispering.

"Made me look bad with the others. Then you go and bring back this joker. Shit, Jodi, that was dumb."

"It was not. It's the only way we're going to get this mess settled and get out of here."

Behind them that loud cackling laughter echoed again. Curry waved up at the open hay loft door and a squirrelly young man appeared and waved back, the knife he'd used to cut the corpse's noose still clutched in his hand.

"C'mon out, boys," Curry said, staring at Cord. "I guess tough ole Diamondback ain't gonna hurt us just yet."

Half a dozen outlaws drifted out into the grey streets, rifles and pistols drawn, but none pointing at any specific target. Cord didn't recognize any of the men, but he recognized the type. Hard, tough faces with wrinkled eyes from squinting down the sights of their guns.

"Over here, Dutch," Curry waved across the street at the squirrelly man emerging from the barn.

Dutch shoved his knife back in its sleeve and came running across the street, his thin lips stretched happily across crooked teeth. His skin was ghostly pale, almost matching that of the corpse on the ground, which he hopped over as if it were nothing more than a mud puddle. At his approach, the other outlaws made room for him, more than was needed, and Cord could see a certain deference and fear for this man.

"Lookee, lookee, lookee," Dutch cackled, adjusting his wire-rim glasses, one lens of which was missing. "We got us a real live judge come to help us poor ignorant sinners learn how to divide." He tipped his hat mockingly. "Surely do appreciate it, Mr. Diamondback. Hope I didn't scare you too much by dropping poor Floyd here on ya." He laughed a mean hacking laugh and patted Cord on the knee.

Cord smiled back, shrugging indifference. Then, as hard as he could, kicked Dutch in the face with his boot. The little man's head snapped back with a nasty crack, lifting him off the ground and slamming him on his back unconscious.

Half a dozen guns swung toward him.

"Gee, I'll have to do something about that nervous twitch in my leg—" Cord started to say, but was interrupted by the whack of a rifle butt smashing into the back of his skull. He tumbled off his horse and kept tumbling down and down and down.

"*Ja*, some big damn help he is." Heavy Swedish accent.

"Shut up, Sven." Woman, to his left.

"I ain't got to shut up, Gretel Peters," the Swede argued. "I ain't got to do nothing."

The woman snorted. " 'Cept what they tell you to do."

Apparently the Swede had no reply to that and merely grumbled and stomped away.

Cord felt a cool hand press against his forehead. He hoped it would stay there for a long time.

"He's looking better, Reverend," the woman said. "Looks to me like he's trying to come out of it."

It suddenly occurred to Cord that they were talking about him and he wondered, come out of what? Then he tried to move his head and felt a floodgate bursting open at the back of his skull, pouring in ton after ton of rushing liquid pain.

"Don't try to move," a man's voice said softly. "Just open your eyes."

Simple enough. Cord tried to open them. Nothing. He concentrated harder. Nothing. He took a deep breath and tried again. Slowly they peeled back, rough and coarse as if there was sand under his eyelids. They raked across the delicate eye until he could see the faces of a man and woman hovering over him. The man was a black-coated reverend, not more than twenty-seven; the woman was a grey-haired grandmother-type in her sixties. They were both smiling.

"Hell of a scare you gave us, Mr. Diamondback," the grandmother said. "Sons of bitches tossed you in here like a sack of feed."

The reverend nodded gravely. "Looks like they may have broken your cheek, too."

"That was from somebody else," Cord explained. "Anything broken?"

"Mrs. Peters?"

The old woman shook her head. "Naw, the bastard's in pretty good shape."

"Well, then maybe you'd help me sit up."

The reverend frowned. "I don't know if that's wise, Mr. Diamondback."

Cord chuckled. "I've done a lot of things the past couple days, Reverend, but being wise hasn't been one of them."

"That's for damn sure," the old lady said. "Otherwise you wouldn't have come here, you dumb bastard."

"Mrs. Peters has divided the world into two groups, Mr. Diamondback," the reverend explained with a smile. "Sons of bitches and bastards."

Mrs. Peters giggled happily at Cord. "The son of a bitch is right."

They each slid an arm under Cord's back and lifted him to a sitting position, his head leaning against the wall. Cord looked around the room slowly. He made no effort to hide his amazement. "Christ, there must be over two hundred of you here."

"Two hundred and sixty-eight," the reverend said.

Cord continued to survey the room. Obviously it was a saloon, or once had been. Now it was a prison meant to hold 268 prisoners. The entire town of Dog Trail.

There was a group of thirty of forty people gathered around Cord, watching him closely, but with no expression on their faces. The rest of the people were milling about, stretched out on their bedrolls, playing cards, or sleeping. They were so tightly packed that it was difficult to move without bumping into someone else.

A flight of stairs near the front door lead up to a balcony that encircled the entire room. Three gunmen were spaced at intervals along the balcony, guarding the crowd. One was napping, tipped back in his chair, his feet resting on the banister, his hat pulled over his eyes. The other two stared at Cord with bored eyes.

"Only three guards?" Cord asked.

"Three's enough," the reverend said.

The old lady hooked a thumb over her shoulder at them. "Those bastards would shoot you down faster than spit on ice if you just go near the door."

A big blonde man in his late fifties who'd been pacing nervously nearby, marched over and joined the conversation. "Maybe Mr. big-deal Diamondback would like us all to get killed trying. *Ja*, Mr. big-deal Diamondback?"

Cord ignored him. "I sure would appreciate a drink of water."

"Of course," the reverend said. "Sister Agnes?"

"Yes, Reverend Kincaid?" a small voice answered from somewhere behind the knot of people gathered around Cord. Then a couple of the people shifted positions and a young woman in a black religious habit nudged through the line. Cord guessed she was in her late twenties, though it was hard to tell because of the veil over her hair. She was pretty, that much was obvious, though she seemed embarrassed by his scrutiny and lowered her head.

"A glass of water for Mr. Diamondback," Reverend Kincaid said. She nodded, almost curtsied, and wedged her way back through the crowd, the floor-length hem of her black frock chasing after her.

"You were supposed to settle this thing," the Swede complained, his blustering face turning red. "That's what everyone said. Settled and then they'd leave us alone."

"Shut up, Sven," the old lady said. "You're the loudest son of a bitch I've ever seen."

"He's right, Gretel," someone in the crowd said. "This fella was supposed to settle things up."

"Excuse me. Excuse me, please," Sister Agnes pleaded quietly as she weaved back through the people. She kneeled next to him and offered the beer mug. Some of the contents had spilled out and beaded on her hand and rolled down her wrist. He noticed a heavy scar there peeking out under her sleeve. "Here's your water, Mr. Diamondback."

"Thanks, Sister Agnes."

She quickly lowered her eyes.

"I don't want to be too personal, Mr. Diamondback," Reverend Kincaid said, "but it's true that there have been rumors for a almost a week now that they were bringing in someone to settle the arguing among these bandits. We had hoped, well, considering your reputation—"

"You've heard of me?"

"Not personally, no. But several others in this room had. Mr. Regvall here."

The big Swede nodded vigorously. "*Ja*, sure, I heard of you. So have a couple of the others. I was a blacksmith in Lincoln when you settled that sheepherders war. Slick piece of business everybody say."

Cord nodded. "Well, I guess this isn't going to be quick as slick."

"What happened?" the old lady asked.

"Seems like hiring me wasn't a unanimous decision. A couple of your friends let me know how un-unanimous it was."

"Which ones?"

" 'Angel Eyes' Curry and a skinny weasel he called Dutch."

The old lady shook her head grimly. "Curry is bad enough, but that Dutch character is just plain crazy. He wouldn't piss on you if you were on fire."

The Swede nodded agreement. "*Ja*, he may be skinny, but Dutch Vries is meaner than a one-legged wolf. Chew your arm off if it suits him."

"He's raped two of the women here already," Reverend Kincaid said. "Beat one near to death."

Cord inched himself further up, ignoring the throbbing at the base of his skull. "I'd appreciate some information."

"Sure," Reverend Kincaid said. "What do you want to know?"

"Everything that happened since they rode in here."

The crowd that had been gathered began to drift away one by one, now that they were certain nothing interesting was going to happen. Most people by now were in their bedrolls, the blankets pulled over their heads to keep out the light from the lamps overhead.

The only ones still clustered around Cord were the Swede, Sven Regvall; Reverend Kincaid; the old lady, Gretel Peters; and Sister Agnes, who sat on the floor behind Reverend Kincaid.

"It all happened pretty fast, really," Reverend Kincaid explained. "They rode in here more than two weeks ago, shot up the place a little, and in less than half an hour they owned this town."

"Didn't anybody fight back?"

"These chickenshit bastards?" the old lady snorted.

"What could we do?" the Swede asked defensively. "They are professionals."

Cord didn't look at him, keeping his gaze on the reverend.

"Mr. Regvall is right. There isn't much that could be done. Most of the men were working their claims, knee-deep in muddy water. By the time they knew what was going on, the outlaws had rounded up most of the women and children."

"Not that it would've mattered much anyway," the old lady said. "This town is long on dreams and short on spine."

"Gretel, that's not fair, by golly," Regvall complained.

"Shut up, Sven."

Reverend Kincaid continued, "They started squabbling amongst themselves almost right away. Victor Curry wanted to kill the men who'd cut off his ear, but the Quinn brothers argued against any killing. They weren't wanted for murder anywhere and they didn't want to start here. Curry let the matter drop until his girlfriend left to get you. Then they hauled Floyd Danby and his partner, Steve Fenedy, out into the street, shot Steve in the head, and cut off poor Floyd's ear and hung him."

"That's not the worst of it, neither," Gretel said. "That son of a bitch Dutch Vries started arranging these combats between the townsfolk. Gladiator fights he called them. Forced Bill Simms to kill Dave Morris with a scythe. It was awful."

"Why do the people go along with it?" Cord asked.

"Don't have no choice. Dutch'd kill them both if they didn't fight each other. This way at least one gets to live."

Cord took a sip of water from the beer mug. He didn't have to look to see his gun was gone, as was the flat throwing knife he'd had strapped to his forearm, and the Remington over-and-under .41 derringer he'd stuffed into his boot before riding into town. Not that they would have done much good against these odds. He'd recognized that as soon as he'd seen the men gathering around his horse a couple hours ago. Kicking Dutch might have seemed foolish to some, but he'd seen right away that Dutch wanted to push him into something right then. It could have ended only one way, with Cord bleeding from a dozen shots while dust blew into his dead staring eyes. By kicking Dutch unconscious, he managed to postpone the confrontation a while.

"I know about Curry and his cousin Ray," Cord said. "And I know that the two Quinn brothers are here. But who's this Dutch Vries? Where does he fit in?"

"He's a son of a bitch," Gretel mumbled.

"Other than that."

Reverend Kincaid looked embarrassed. "Well, he's Tom Delancy's ramrod, second in command of the gang."

"He is more than that," the Swede said with disgust.

"Yes, well," Reverend Kincaid reddened. "He seems to also have a special relationship with Delancy."

"Special, *ja*."

Gretel chuckled. "They're trying to tell you he's queer. The two of them sleep together."

"He's the same one that raped two of your women?"

"Hell," Gretel said, "Dutch would screw a hitching rail if it moved in the wind."

"Enough, Gretel," Reverend Kincaid said, looking protectively at Sister Agnes, who huddled behind him, her head buried in her knees.

Gretel slapped her thigh and laughed. "Men have such trouble talking about these things. Why is that, Diamondback?"

Cord couldn't help but smile at her. "Beats me."

"Anyway," Reverend Kincaid continued quickly, "they've all been at each other's throats ever since the first day they got here. Mostly about how to split up everything they've stolen from us. Delancy and Dutch want the split to be divided equally among each man. Because they brought the others here, Curry and his cousin want to take half for themselves and let Delancy and the Quinns divide the rest. The Quinns think it ought to be a three-way split among the three gangs."

"How much money they talking about?"

"Including the gold, horses, silverware, and anything else they could find, about $60,000."

"Not bad."

"And until they decide how to split, they've got the men working their claims during the days while they keep everyone else locked up here. So the pot gets bigger."

"Aren't they worried about visitors?"

Gretel looked shocked. "Visitors? To Dog Trail?

This ain't a place people come to, mister, it's a place to leave."

"She's right," Reverend Kincaid acknowledged. "When there was a lot of gold up here, Dog Trail had five thousand people living here. But the mother-lode tapped out five years ago and it's taken that long to whither down to this size. Those that stay work their placers hoping picking up just enough to get by, hoping to find another vein of gold."

"All the real prospectors is gone," Gretel said, a note of lament in her voice. "They could see this place weren't good for nothing no more. What we got now are storekeepers, retired cowboys, losers who failed at everything else until they worked their way down to Dog Trail."

Reverend Kincaid didn't say anything, but Cord could tell from his expression that he agreed with the old woman's assessment.

"Maybe you're right, Gretel," the Swede said, "but it's not our fault. We try to do good, make a living. It's just not fair what happened to us."

"Stop whining, Sven," Gretel said. "You see, Diamondback, that's what most of the town's like. Whining and snivelling about what's fair and just. They got some learning to do, don't they?"

"Why do you stay, Gretel?" Cord asked.

She smiled, flashing a set of perfect teeth between wrinkled old lips. "Business, son. If these fools are gonna stay here and scratch for gold—which most of them are too dumb to recognize anyway—somebody's got to supply them."

"And what do you supply them with?"

Her smiled widened to include pink gums. "Girls. I run the only brothel in town. Of course, Delancy has all my girls across the street at my place. Using them all for free." She shook her head sadly. "Talk about injustice."

Cord looked at the reverend. "So Delancy's men are staying across the street at Gretel's place. Where are the others?"

"We're on a cross street," he said, drawing a cross in the air. "On the bottom right corner is us, Fancy Dan's Saloon. Above us across Nugget Street, is Gretel's, uh, place with Delancy's gang. To the left of them is the only saloon in town that was still open, Owl Creek Saloon. That's where Curry and his cousin stay. And across the street next to us at Fenster's Hotel are the Quinn brothers. They stay pretty much to themselves. They've tried to prevent most of the violence that's occurred so far, including the horrible gladiator fights that Dutch stages. But without much luck."

"And the gangs are all still fighting amongst themselves?"

"Yes, worse than ever. A few days ago one of Delancy's men threatened Ulysses Quinn with a knife. Quinn broke his arm. They almost shot it out over that."

"Sometimes I wish they would," Gretel said.

Cord shook his head. "That wouldn't help. It'd only make things worse for you. So far they've kept each other in check for the most part. I'd hate to think what would happen if there was a shootout and Delancy and Dutch won. You people would be in worse shape."

"What are we going to do?" Sven Regvall asked. "We can't keep going like this. Can you help us?"

Cord stared at him with a cold and stony gaze. Finally, the big Swede turned away.

Reverend Kincaid broke into the uneasy silence

with a forced cough. "I think we'd better let Mr. Diamondback get some rest. That's quite a nasty crack on the back of your head."

Cord had to admit he was hurting. The pain in his head had progressed from dull throbbing to a kind of fiery squeezing around his temples. A little sleep would do him a lot of good. Tomorrow, and the dangers it brought, would come soon enough.

" 'Night, son," Gretel said, turning and picking her way roughly through the prone bodies of the sleeping townspeople.

Sven Regvall looked sunken and frightened as he hunched away without a word, stealing nervous glances at the guards above.

"Goodnight, Reverend," Sister Agnes said, then added, her eyes darting to the floor, "Goodnight, Mr. Diamondback. God bless."

"Thank you, Sister," Cord smiled, but she hurried off before seeing it.

"We have a little corner to ourselves near the storeroom," Reverend Kincaid said, pointing at the far wall.

"That was nice of everyone."

Reverend Kincaid smiled. "Yes, though I think the motivation was more practical. Most people are nervous when sleeping near 'religious' persons."

Cord laughed quietly, as not disturb those sleeping around him. "I see what you mean. Still, the two of you make an unusual combination."

"Yes, you mean because she's a Catholic sister and I'm a Methodist minister."

Cord nodded. "Not to mention her exceptional good looks."

Reverend Kincaid grinned sheepishly, looking even younger. "Well, I have to admit to noticing *that*

myself. Not that it means any disrespect toward those
of the calling, but my usual experience with women
willing to become that devout is that they are, um,
perhaps a bit, well, homely." He seemed thoughtful
for a moment. "But Sister Agnes has had special
hardships. Having lost both parents when she was a
only ten, she soon found herself employed as a,
uh . . ." He sighed uncomfortably.

"Prostitute."

He shrugged. "After being sold from one house to
another, she finally tried to commit suicide by slashing her wrists. Perhaps you noticed the scars."

Cord nodded.

"Fortunately, she was taken in by a priest and
shortly afterwards decided to take her vows. I met
her several months ago in Denver. She was awaiting
the arrival of a priest whom she was to accompany to
Dog Trail to establish a Roman Catholic church. I
was scouting locations for a church over in Leadville.
She received a wire informing her of her party's
indeterminate delay and I sort of, well, looked after a
bit. Finally she convinced me that we could come up
here together and start one church together, just
dividing it in half." He smiled broadly. "The idea
appealed to me and here we are, still trying to decide
what land to buy. She works like an angel trying to
find the right location, but she's so naive. She wants
a big parcel of land further up the hill because it
would be a shining tribute to God. Unfortunately I
had to explain the harsh realities. Shining tribute or
not, we needed something people didn't have to trek
up muddy or icy roads to get to. Poor child."

Cord's head had shifted from squeezing to pounding now and he felt his eyes slipping closed as the
reverend talked on. Somehow the drone of the young

man's pleasant voice eased Cord toward sleep. When Reverend Kincaid seemed to flag, Cord asked, "Tell me about some of the members of Delancy's gang."

"Well, there's Reno Hernandez, Mexican . . ." And on he talked until Cord could barely hear him. He seemed to be drifting further and further away, sinking to the bottom of a dark lake. Somewhere down there he thought he saw Jodi, swimming naked, her smooth breasts rippling with the current. When he heard the first screams, he pushed toward consciousness, swimming for the surface, his legs kicking, his breath bursting in his lungs. Finally, he broke through, just in time for the first gunshot. And a woman's screams.

17.

Reverend Kincaid must have nodded off next to Diamondback, because he was just blinking his eyes open while Cord was leaping to his feet. The sudden movement tripped the sleeping pain at the back of his head. As he ran toward the screaming, he could feel it pushing on the inside of his skull from all directions as if it wanted to burst out.

The guards at the balcony were already on their feet with guns drawn yelling for everyone to sit still. Most people obliged, content to knuckle eye sockets, yawn, and mumble questions about what might be happening.

But not Cord. He dodged and leaped over people at a speed that didn't permit politeness. Occasionally he had to shove a curious citizen down on their butts, or shoulder them aside into their neighbor's bedroll.

He could tell by the gathered blockade of people where the action was taking place, though he still couldn't see who was involved. But he did recognize one voice. Sister Agnes.

Out of the corner of his eye he saw two of the guards, pistols waving townspeople out of their way, picking their way through the crowd toward the scene of the commotion. One of them, who the reverend had identified as Gypsy Smith, kicked a slow-moving old man in the face, sending him sprawling into a sitting woman.

Cord finally hurdled the last row of bedrolls and dove between the watching crowd, elbowing them roughly aside. When he broke through, he saw what all the screaming was about. Anger shivered through his body like an Arctic wind.

Dutch Vries hovered over Sister Agnes, who was flat on her back trying to kick him away. Her black habit was torn down the front, exposing her large soft breasts. She tried to cover them with one arm, while continuing to fight him off with the other. But Dutch just cackled, his lips loose from drinking, his mouth drooling from lust. Under his chin was a long dark bruise where Cord had kicked him earlier. In his right fist he clutched a Colt Frontier double-action .45, which he pointed at the ceiling and fired twice. At the sound the line of observers backed up a few steps.

Dutch holstered his gun, drunkenly grabbed Sister Agnes's churning legs forcing them to spread apart. The heavy skirt of her habit slid down her long trim legs and bunched around her hips. She wore only thin white underpants beneath. Dutch dropped to his knees, his elbows hooked around her thighs, prying them apart. Quickly he fumbled open his trousers and began pulling at her underpants with one hand and grabbing her exposed breasts with the other.

"Dear God, please," she sobbed, pushing at him while trying to hold on her panties. But even drunk Dutch was too powerful and he tore them off with ease.

Cord could hear Reno Hernandez and Gypsy Smith bullying their way through the crowd. If he was going to do anything it was now or never. He had no illusions about receiving help from the townspeople, they were too frightened to help themselves let alone anyone else. Gretel had been right about them. They were losers at everything who'd finally settled in Dog Trail the way silt settles at the bottom of water. They forever complained about how unfairly life had treated them, about their bad luck. But they were incapable of doing anything about it.

"Hold still ya fucking bitch," Dutch cackled, slapping Sister Agnes across the face.

The crowd gasped with shock. Cord Diamondback ran two steps and dove through the air. His outstretched arms encircled Dutch's surprised face and he wrenched him roughly from atop Sister Agnes. There wasn't much of a fight; Cord snapped three rapid jabs into Dutch's jaw, using the bruise as a target. Dutch's head bounced off the floor each time. His hand squirmed toward his holster, but Cord's knee quickly pinned the wrist to the floor. He rammed his other knee between Dutch's legs. Dutch coughed in pain, his body curling from the impact.

"Get out of the way, assholes," Reno Hernandez shouted as he and the Gypsy Smith pushed their way to the front of the crowd. When he saw what was going on, he barked, "Oh, shit!" and aimed his gun at Cord's back.

Cord saw them both taking aim and started rolling off Dutch. But he had barely moved when the shots echoed through the room.

Cord expected to be dead when the last echo died, but he wasn't. He kept rolling and saw why. Reverend Kincaid had jumped the two guards from behind, knocking their aim wild. But that ploy was only good once, when you had surprise on your side.

Now the two gunmen were swinging their pistols on the reverend.

Cord hopped to his feet and dashed toward the outlaws. The crowd of people stumbled over each other to get out of the way, like scared sheep in a chute.

"Hold it, Diamondback!" a raspy voice shouted.

Everyone stopped moving. Cord turned to face the voice. Dutch Vries was on his knees, his Colt aimed directly at Cord's forehead. His hand shook slightly from anger, and his thin lips stretched across a grim mouth. His glasses were cocked awkwardly on his face and he used his free hand to straighten them. He climbed to his feet, a little hunched over from the damage to his crotch. Without a word, he walked over to Reverend Kincaid, who was still sitting where he'd fallen after tackling the two gunmen. Dutch smiled cruelly at Reverend Kincaid and suddenly lashed the barrel of his pistol across the reverend's forehead. The reverend moaned once and fell back unconscious, a long ugly gash just below his hairline.

Dutch spun around to face Cord, his gun twitching anxiously in his hand. "Tough guy, eh, Diamondback? Like to fight? Why don't you do something now?"

Cord stared impassively.

"Huh? C'mon now, partner. Let's see your stuff." As he spoke, Dutch's confidence began to build again. He enjoyed the attention of the crowd, their fear so thick Cord could smell it. They were afraid to look at him, afraid not to. "Big men came to set us all straight." Dutch spit on the unconscious reverend. "Ain't that right, Diamondback? What kinda name is that anyway. Diamondback. Sounds like a fucking squaw name. Is that what you are, Diamondass, a squaw?" He stepped up to Cord and shoved his gun in Cord's face, tapping the barrel lightly against Cord's fractured cheek. Each tap became harder and harder until Cord had to force himself not to wince from the pain. "Answer me, Diamonddick. You got a squaw name?"

Cord said nothing. He merely lowered his eyes into Dutch's, drilling into them. Dutch stared back at first, his squirrelly face sneering over the barrel of his pistol. But as they continued to lock stares, Dutch's face began to sag and something like fear began to etch across his features. He seemed to become aware of it all at once and suddenly clubbed Cord on the shoulder with his gun. Cord dropped to his knees clutching his shoulder.

Dutch shook a finger in Cord's face. "You like to fight so much, asshole, we're gonna give you a chance. Tomorrow morning you're gonna get a taste of real fighting. Gladiator style." He glanced over at Sister Agnes who had rearranged her clothing to cover her exposed body. Then he curled his lip in contempt and waved for the two gunmen to return to their posts. He shoved and kicked his way to the front door, turning to face Cord after he unlocked it. "You'll like our little arena, Diamondback. You'll like it to death." He hurried out the door, relocking it. But everyone could still hear his cackling laughter as it drifted tauntingly through the room. They all turned to face Cord, staring at him with a mixture of fear and pity.

As if looking at a dead man.

18.

Everyone was there.

Waiting.

Waiting for it to begin.

Cord squinted out through the bright early-morning sun and studied the corrupt faces that gathered like hungry wolves for the spectacle. He recognized most of the outlaws from either their wanted posters or from descriptions that Reverend Kincaid gave him last night.

Leaning against the Owl Creek Saloon was Victor "Angel Eyes" Curry, puffing on a fat cigar that only looked foolish in his youthful face. His cousin Ray had his arms hooked over the batwing doors and was rocking back and forth on them. He looked to be a couple years older than his cousin, with a full black beard that seemed somehow to annoy Victor.

The Quinn brothers sat in wooden rocking chairs in front of the hotel, sipping coffee and finishing what looked, by the stack of dishes piled in front of them, to be a large breakfast. Ulysses Quinn was the older brother, mid-thirties with a bushy red Viking beard streaked with grey. Jason Quinn was two years younger but thirty pounds heavier and four inches taller than his brother. He was wearing a fancy tweed suit complete with white shirt and string tie. The brothers chatted quietly with each other, seeming to ignore the hoopla around them.

Over at Gretel's cathouse, Tom Delancy and his gang were standing around the hitching posts passing bottles of whiskey around, squeezing three tired-looking whores. There were nine of them, including Delancy, who stood in the middle like the captain of an elite squad. Delancy was a short man, shorter than any of his men, but he had a broad barrel chest and thick stumpy legs that carried a lot of authority. He also had a reputation for being damned fast with that Colt he wore cross-rigged on his hip. He was maybe thirty years old, the oldest one in his gang. His eyes were a flat green, like a stagnant pond, but there was a cleverness there too. Calculating.

The rest of his gang took their cue from him. Reno Hernandez, the Mexican who was known to be good with knives; Short-Spear Dugan, the half-Apache Irishman; Dummy, who stood almost seven feet tall but was mentally retarded. And there were the defectors, former members of Curry's gang: Billy Faro, sixteen years old and couldn't keep his hands off his gun; Gypsy Smith, blonde, carefully handsome; Grover Benson, his arm wrapped and splinted where Ulysses Quinn had broken it during their recent argument; and Felix Clark, an Englishman who'd run away from a good family to be an American outlaw.

Cord took off his hat and wiped his forehead with his sleeve. They all looked the same to him: cynical, arrogant, short-tempered.

Behind him, strung out along the street in front of Fancy Dan's Saloon, were all the townspeople, herded out at gunpoint to watch.

"Where you want the body shipped?" Victor Curry laughed. At that moment, Jodi forced her way passed

Ray, brushing through the batwing doors and out into the street. She stared wearily at Cord, not trying to hide her concern anymore. Curry circled her waist as she ran by and hauled her in next to him, laughing and kissing her cheek. She didn't fight him, offering her cheek and neck, but never taking her eyes off Cord.

Cord looked over his shoulder and saw Sister Agnes politely excusing herself to everyone as she edged through the crowd.

"How's the reverend?" Cord asked.

"Still out, but breathing restfully."

Cord nodded and looked around the square again. Dutch Vries was still nowhere in sight.

"Hey," Tom Delancy called, cupping his hands around his mouth. "You Quinn brothers too good for this? Hope we ain't offending your delicate morals, boys." His gang laughed dutifully and slopped down more whiskey.

Ulysses Quinn stood up, his red beard reflecting sparks from the morning sun. "My brother and I are businessmen, Delancy. We didn't come here to play kids' games. We came here for money. That's what you and Curry promised when we joined you."

"And that's what you'll get," Delancy said. "Your fair share."

"We don't like your idea of fair. Maybe if someone in your ignorant little gang knew how to add without taking off their shoes, we'd feel better."

Delancy took a couple angry steps forward and rested his hand on his Colt. "Anytime you want to settle it, Quinn." Delancy's men all shifted, pushing women aside and setting down bottles, to free their gun hands.

Ulysses Quinn laughed deeply. "We aren't idiots,

Delancy. There's only two of us. But we're willing to do what's necessary to get what's coming to us."

Victor Curry unwrapped his arm from Jodi and yelled across the street. "Hell, you Quinns got nothing to bitch about. It was me and Ray that set this whole thing up. I'm the one that brought you all here. I'm the one that had my fucking ear cut off." He turned his head and lifted the bandanna. A small tab of ear and lobe was all that remained.

Jason Quinn called back, "Seems to me your brain needed the extra air."

Diamondback took a few steps into the street. "Looks to me like you boys could use me after all."

The reply came from over his shoulder. "We're gonna use you all right. My way." Dutch Vries drew his Colt. "Keep walking, Diamondback."

Cord walked into the center of the intersection, an equal distance from each group.

Dutch holstered his Colt and began addressing everyone, walking around Cord in a circle as he spoke. " 'Friends, Romans, countrymen, lend me your ear . . .' " He turned to Victor Curry. "Of course 'Angel Eyes' here's already gone and lent his out." Delancy and his gang laughed wildly. Even some of the townspeople giggled.

"Shut up, Dutch, you bastard," Curry growled.

Dutch cackled happily, the sun glinting off the one lens in his glasses. "Now, last night I promised you another of my famous sporting events and as you can see I am keeping my promise." Delancy's gang applauded and whistled. "Thank you. Since we took this town the way the Romans used to conquer towns, we deserve the same kinda entertainment they used to have. Gladiator fights." He spun back toward Cord. "Ready?"

"Who do I fight?"

He grinned wolfishly. "Me."

"Then I'm ready."

Dutch's grin widened. "And Dummy."

Dummy lumbered down from the porch, his seven feet and three hundred pounds unnervingly solid. His mouth hung open in a perpetual expression of confusion. "What d'ya want me to do, Dutch?"

"Kill him." He pointed at Cord.

"Okay," Dummy shrugged good-naturedly and started toward Cord.

"No, no. Not yet. Not barehanded. First the weapons." Dutch walked over to his horse opened the saddlebag. He dipped in and pulled out a rusty-edged hatchet, tossing it on the ground near Dummy's feet. "That's for you. A present from me, Dummy."

Dummy smiled happily as he scooped it up, examining it closely. "Thanks a lot, Dutch."

Delancy's gang howled with laughter, slapping each other on the back.

"Get on with it, Dutch," Tom Delancy said.

"Sure, Tom." Dutch reached into the bag again and pulled out a straight razor. Slowly he opened it, letting the sun skate along its bright blade. "Don't you worry none, Mr. Diamondback. I'm only gonna take a little off around the edges. Of your neck." He cackled again, slapping his knee.

"What about him?" Jodi yelled, breaking away from Curry's arm and running into the street. "What weapon does he have?"

Dutch snapped his fingers. "Almost forgot. Now you don't think I wouldn't keep this on and up and up, do ya little lady?" He reached into the saddle bag and pulled out a wooden gavel and lofted it toward Cord, who caught it in mid-air. "He's a judge, so I figured he should feel right at home with it. Took me most of the morning to find one in this damned town. Suit you okay, Diamondback?"

Cord clenched the wooden gavel in his right hand. He leveled his dark eyes on Dutch and watched that same wave of fear wash over his squirrelly features. Cord smiled. "Let's go."

"Yeah," Delancy's gang shouted. "Do it to 'em, Dutch."

Dutch shook off whatever feeling of anxiety he had and started toward Cord in a slow stalking move-ment, his arms wide, the razor extended in his right hand. "C'mon, Dummy, let's get him."

Dummy nodded and imitated Dutch's movements, only using his hatchet. His movements were slow and clumsy, but there was enough power in him to cleave Cord in half with one swipe.

Cord backed up cautiously, glancing over his shoul-der at Jodi. "Get off the street. Move."

"Oh, God, Cord, I'm sorry," she sobbed. "I'm so damned sorry."

Then Curry grabbed her roughly around her arm and yanked her off the street.

"What's the matter, Curry?" Delancy taunted. "First you lose your ear, then you lose your girl."

Curry shoved Jodi against the wall, knocking the wind out of her. "Just stand there and shut up," he hissed.

Dutch shuffled closer and closer, tossing the razor from one hand to the other. "You wanted me," he rasped, "now come and get me."

Cord tucked the gavel handle in his belt and took a boxing stance. Bouncing up on his toes, he moved quickly in an arc away from Dutch and toward Dummy.

"Get him, Dummy," Dutch said.

Dummy nodded, his face taut with concentration. He raised the hatchet over his head and charged at Cord, chopping the air between them as if it were jungle he had to clear. Cord slipped to the left just as the heavy blade whooshed past his ear. Quickly he hooked a fist up into Dummy's jaw. Dummy staggered back a step, shook his head once and smiled. Then he charged forward again, chopping the air with new vigor.

In the meantime, Dutch had maneuvered around, trying to trap Cord between himself and Dummy. But Cord danced away again, using Dummy as a shield from Dutch. Dummy hoisted the hatchet high over his head again and brought it whistling down toward Cord's neck. Cord jumped back, but not before the edge of the rusty blade snagged his shirt, slicing a ragged line down the front. Cord could feel a bubble of blood trickling down his chest.

He wouldn't be able to keep this up indefinitely. Soon Dutch would become frustrated and resort to a less showy way of killing him.

Dummy was being more cautious now in his attacks, not wanting to be laughed at any more for missing. He waded in, his shoulders hunched, his meaty hands wrapped around the small wooden handle. His tongue was lodged in the corner of his mouth in concentration.

Cord stopped moving, allowing Dummy to catch up. A smile of satisfaction spread across the boy's flaccid face as he came within striking distance. The hatchet was poised over his shoulder in the stance of a lumberjack. He grit his teeth and swung it down toward Cord's head. At the last second, Diamondback rolled to the left, pumping two solid punches into Dummy's jaw. Dummy frowned at the pain, but otherwise seemed unaffected as he pivoted around. Cord quickly sank two more shots into Dummy's kidney. Dummy grunted and grabbed his side.

"Get the bastard!" Gretel Peters hollered, shaking her fist. "Get him, Diamondback."

A murmur of approval fluttered through the crowd of imprisoned townspeople.

"Get out of the way, Dummy," Dutch shrieked, advancing with his razorblade flashing in the sun.

But Dummy didn't hear him. He was wondering why Cord had been able to do what no one else had ever been able to do: hurt him with a punch. If only he'd stand still, he'd show him. He stumbled after Cord, the hatchet dangling at his side.

Cord dove at Dummy's feet, bowling them out from under him. Dummy's arms flew into the air as he flopped forward on his face, his open mouth scooping a mound of dirt. The hatchet somersaulted to the ground three feet away. He started to push himself back to his feet when he felt two knees crashing into his back, slamming his face back into the dirt.

Over his shoulder, Cord could see Dutch rushing toward him. There was no more time to lose with this boy, though he didn't want to kill him, not in his state of mind. Instead he whipped out the wooden gavel from his belt and pounded Dummy's skull twice before he had to dive off to avoid the slashing razor of Dutch. But twice had been enough, and a loud splatter of applause filled the air as the townspeople realized Dummy was unconscious.

Cord rolled off Dummy's back and kept rolling until he'd grabbed the loose hatchet from the ground. When he sprang to his feet again, he was armed with the gavel in his left hand and the hatchet in the right.

Dutch halted and licked his suddenly dry lips. "Dummy," he called, nudging the fallen ox with his foot. "*Dummy!*"

"Appears you're all alone now, Dutch," Ulysses Quinn goaded. "Let's see what you can do."

Reno Hernandez let his hand drift quietly toward his gun but Tom Delancy stopped him with a restraining touch.

Sweat popped out all over Dutch's high forehead, and he swiped at it with his free hand. "I'm gonna cut you, Diamondback. Cut you bad."

Cord made a sudden lunging motion and shouted, "Boo!"

Dutch stumbled backwards, tripping over his feet and falling hard on his butt.

The townspeople, the Currys, and the Quinns all laughed. A couple of titters even rippled through Delacy's gang.

"Give it up, Dutch," Tom Delancy advised with concern. "We don't need this. Use your gun."

"Fuck off!" Dutch screamed, scurrying to his feet. "I'll kill him my way." Dutch's eyes bulged with fury as he waded toward Cord, the razor no longer flipping from hand to hand. Firmly planted in his right fist. "It's your balls now, Diamondback," he spit.

Cord glided backwards, allowing Dutch to build a momentum. Each step Dutch took, he moved with more speed and less caution. Within seconds he was practically trotting after the back-pedalling Cord.

Then Diamondback started moving forward.

This confused Dutch and he immediately slashed out clumsily at Cord with the razor. Cord caught the

wrist in the crook of the gavel, twisted sharply until
he heard the wrist snap and Dutch howl with pain.
The razor dropped harmlessly in the dirt.

For a long moment Cord studied the snarling face
before him, the teeth bared in haste, the eye behind
the one lens magnified to a giant portrait of evil.
Dutch screeched a litany of profanity at Cord and
fumbled for his Colt with his left hand.

Cord waited no longer.

He swung the hatchet in a straight screaming line
until it sank into the top of Dutch's head with a
sickening crack. Blood gushed up in thick inky
geysers as Dutch fell silent in mid-curse and fell
limply to the ground. His sphincter and bladder relaxed and the dead man fouled himself as he lay there
twitching and pumping blood into the dirt.

There was a long hard silence. Nobody moved.
Nobody spoke.

Then Tom Delancy shuffled forward, his skin
drained of all blood, his face twisted into a knot of
intense pain and hate. He lifted his stagnant green
eyes from Dutch's body to Cord, drew his Colt, and
pointed it at Cord's head. *"Die, you son of a bitch!"* he
screamed. *"Die!"*

19.

There's nowhere to hide from a .45 slug when you're standing in the middle of an empty street. But Cord would try. He tensed his muscles for a dive at Dutch's body and the Colt still holstered there. The rest of Delancy's gang would probably open fire the minute he moved, but Cord would be damned if was going to stand there and be gunned down without a fight. Delancy grit his teeth with hate and brought his pistol up for a better aim.

"You squeeze that trigger and I'll kill you, Tom Delancy."

Delancy pivoted around to meet the threatening voice.

Jodi walked slowly forward, the fancy Peacemaker .45 swivel rig gripped in her hand and pointing at Delancy's chest.

Reno Hernandez snapped out his gun and aimed it at Jodi.

"He pulls that trigger," she warned in a steady voice, "and you die too."

Delancy stared at her a few moments, weighing his passion to revenge Dutch's death with his desire to save his own life. He was, after all, a practical man. "C'mon now, Jodi, this ain't no fight of yours." He smiled, and the face that just moments before had been twisted in bloodlust was now cheerfully charming. Cord could see how he'd managed to survive this long as an outlaw.

"This is nobody's fight," she said. "We're supposed to be dividing the money and getting the hell out of here. Not playing silly games. Eventually there's bound to be someone coming up here that you won't catch and who'll bring a posse. There was already a bounty hunter trailing Vic."

Delancy took a cautious step toward her, his gun lowered slightly. "Maybe you're right, Jodi. Maybe we have been playing around here too long, letting Dutch have his way. Hell, I know we can work something out."

Jodi looked relieved. "Good, then let's start talk—"

Victor Curry had sneaked up behind Jodi and grabbed her gun hand away with a wrenching twist. She screamed in pain as he shoved it high up between her shoulder blades. "I told you to stay out of this, damn it. Why can't you act like a woman."

Delancy swung around toward Cord, who had quietly inched his way near Dutch's body. Delancy immediately recognized Cord's goal and the charming expression twisted into his former mask of hate.

Cord looked at Delancy's men drawing their guns too. He didn't have a chance now. If you're going to die, he thought with amusement, there's nothing to do but dive straight into hell.

He dove for the gun on Dutch's body.

The explosion of bullets chattered through the morning air.

As Diamondback thudded against Dutch's body, he expected to see his chest torn away. Or at least rivers of blood.

"All right, everybody relax. That means you too, Diamondback."

Cord lifted his head to stare at the speaker. Ulysses

Quinn waved his smoking pistol back and forth, gesturing for everyone to holster their guns. Everyone did, reluctantly. Jason Quinn stood behind his brother, flicking a speck of dirt from his new suit.

"I think you can let the lady go now, Curry," Ulysses said, his voice edged with ice.

Jodi shook loose, rubbing her sore arm and cursing Curry. "How could you, Vic?" she sobbed. "I'm on your side. I'm your girl."

Those words scraped against Cord's insides, but he ignored that. Right now he was deciding whether to keep reaching for Dutch's gun, or wait to see what the Quinns had in mind here. He decided to wait.

Ulysses Quinn stepped into the street scratching his thick red beard. "Seems to me we've fiddled around here enough. Me and Jason have tried to be patient with you all, but being patient goes against our nature. I have to admit, we haven't been pleased from the start. When we joined up with you, Curry here promised us a lot of gold. But most of what we got so far has been life savings of these people, not gold. There's precious little of that around here."

"Hell, they musta hid it somewhere," Victor Curry explained. "Same place they hid Ray's and my gold. The gold they stole from us that night they run us outta town."

A murmur of protested innocence rose from the gathered townspeople.

"There ain't no more gold," Gretel Peters called out. "At least not enough for any real prospectors to fuss up here. Why do you think this town's shrunk so, you stupid bastards!"

"She's lying," Curry said.

"About what?" Ulysses Quinn chuckled. "About the gold or you being a bastard?"

Curry bristled. "Both, damn you. There's plenty of gold. Me and Ray and Jodi dug up lots. Ain't that right?" He swiveled his head between Jodi and Ray.

"That's right," Ray said.

Jodi nodded sadly. "Yes."

"No it's not," Cord said, standing up.

"What the fuck do you know?" Curry snapped. "You weren't even there."

"I know that what Gretel Peters says makes a lot of sense. Except for some meager panning the gold's been picked clean around here. Anyone can see that the people here know just little enough about mining to keep doing it, but not enough to get out."

There was some angry mumbles from the insulted townspeople.

Cord ignored them. "And I know that when we were on the trail here and Jodi described what they'd been panning before they'd been run out of town, it wasn't gold that the three of them had."

"You don't know shit, mister," Curry screamed, practically frothing at the mouth. "How the hell do you know what we had. You weren't even there."

"Gold interests me."

Jodi smiled.

"Go on, Mr. Diamondback," Ulysses Quinn urged.

"Well, Jodi described what they'd been gathering for all those weeks as 'winking and sparkling' in the sun."

Gretel Peters burst out laughing, slapping her thigh. "Hell, gold don't do that."

"Exactly. Real gold looks the same from any angle. But mica and pyrites wink and sparkle when struck by light."

Curry shrieked harshly, "That's not so at all, we—"

"Shut up, Curry," Tom Delancy barked and Victor

Curry fell silent. Delancy stared at Cord. "What about them cutting off his ear and tar-and-feathering Ray?"

"When Ray and Victor had their 'gold' assayed, they were told it wasn't gold at all, but fool's gold. So they stole some from Floyd and his partner. That's one of the reasons he wanted them dead as soon as possible after coming back. Not that he had to, they were both probably too frightened to ever say anything even if they knew what he'd told you. But 'Angel Eyes' just didn't want to take any chances."

"That ain't so!" Curry hollered. "Those sons of bitches cut my damn ear off."

"For stealing their gold. They didn't have much anyway, so they tended to be a might harsh when what little they had was stolen."

There was a tense silence while everyone stared at Victor Curry. He licked his lips and took a few steps backwards.

Cord sleeved the sweat from his brow. "But lying comes natural to Mr. Curry. Certainly he's had enough practice, considering how he's lied all these years about his brother and father."

"What do you mean?" Curry asked.

"I mean you killed your father and brother, branded them to death." He shrugged. "Not that it matters much, but I like to keep the record straight."

"No, Vic," Jodi gasped, backing away in shock. "You didn't do that. You couldn't. I know you've done some mean things, but they made you by not believing your story. I know that."

Curry looked back around at each of the outlaws. That damned Diamondback had made him look like such a kid in front of everybody. They'd laughed at him, just as they'd done with Dutch. But he could see a new respect in the eyes of some of Delancy's men now, especially among those that used to ride with him.

"Yeah," he smirked cockily, "I killed them both."

"God, no," Jodi sobbed.

"Why the fuck not? The old man had money stashed someplace on that farm and wasn't going to give me a cent. Even when I said I was riding out on my own. He said all the money was for the farm. If I wanted to stay on the farm then I would be entitled to it the same as my brother, who'd already decided to be a farmer. A *farmer*." He spit.

Everyone stood transfixed as Curry, his eyes ablaze, recounted the horrible story.

"I was just gonna scare him, that's all. I grabbed the gun and tied 'em both up. But still the old fart wouldn't talk. I hit him a lot, but he just stared at me with those big dumb farmer's eyes. Finally, I got the branding iron out and, just to scare him, threatened my brother with it unless he talked. He said he didn't think anyone who came from his loins could do anything that cruel." Curry laughed. "He was wrong. I was only going to do it once, then if he wouldn't talk I'd just clear out with that spare cash I could get around the house. The hell with 'em both. I pressed the glowing bar to his flesh and it sizzled and bubbled into a blister. The smell was awful, worse than a calf. He screamed something fierce and my father spit in my face. I don't know, after that it was easier, and I did it again and again. I can hardly remember what happened. All I know is that suddenly my brother was dead and there was no turning back."

"Jesus, Vic," Ray Curry said. "I liked them. They were nice. For Christ's sake." He stumbled back into a chair.

"Well, well," Ulysses Quinn grinned thinly. "I think we've been misled by our friend."

Tom Delancy nodded disgustedly. "Yeah. I ought to kill you right now, Curry. All three of you."

Curry sneered, his confidence restored from the glimmers of fear and respect flickering across the outlaw faces. "I don't see what you're bellyaching about, Tom. You neither, Quinn. I brought you here. Maybe there wasn't as much gold as I promised, but you expected I was exaggerating some anyway, right? Hell, that's the nature of this business."

No one disagreed.

Encouraged by their silence, Curry continued, "But we got nearly $60,000 worth of cash and goods here. And we didn't lose one man. We've had a safe place to hide out complete with plenty of food, booze, and women. Shit, I done right by you fellas."

Delancy holstered his gun. "Can't argue that."

Ulysses Quinn nodded. "Maybe not. But I've had it with the company around here. I say we settle it once and for all."

Delancy eased around, his fingers drumming against his holster. "Got any suggestions, Ulysses?"

"As a matter of fact, I do." He holstered his gun but let his hand rest on the butt. "I think Mr. Diamondback here has shown himself to be a shrewd and resourceful man, certainly equal to his sterling reputation. Since he's here anyway, we should take advantage of his skills as an arbitrator."

Delancy frowned. "What if none of us like his decision?"

"Well, then we're back where we started and nobody's lost anything."

"Except him," Delancy said. "He loses his life."

"Suits me," Ulysses said.

"Me too," Jason agreed.

"I don't know," Delancy grimaced. "He killed Dutch."

"We share your grief at the loss of your friend, Tom," Ulysses nodded, "but this is business."

Delancy glanced over at the crumpled corpse on the ground. "Yeah, you're right. Business. I'll go along. He's got one day. Curry?"

Victor Curry looked coldly at Cord. He didn't like it, but he was in no position to go against both gangs. "Okay. One day."

"Mr. Diamondback," Ulysses smiled. "Can you do the job in one day?"

Cord studied the hard faces staring at him. "Sure. But I get $5,000 in cash off the top and my guns."

Delancy balked. "Five thousand! Forget it. Not for one day's work."

Ulysses Quinn nodded. "That is awfully high."

"Well, seeing how we're all such good friends, I'll make it $3,500 and a room of my own."

Quinn and Delancy exchanged expressions without speaking or moving.

"Agreed," Ulysses said. "And you are welcome to stay at our hotel."

"My guns."

There was a pause as Delancy thought it over. Finally he snapped his fingers and Reno Hernandez grudgingly withdrew Cord's gun from his belt and tossed it through the air. Cord caught it, examined it, and slid it into his holster.

"Now, the first thing I want to do is—"

The woman's high-pitched scream came from the behind the crowd of townspeople. Everyone turned to face Sister Agnes as she ran out of Fancy Dan's Saloon, her arms flailing, a bloody knife clutched awkwardly in her hand. "Reverend Kincaid!" she choked. "He's dead."

20.

"I killed him," she sobbed.

Cord patted her hand as they walked.

"It's true," she said. "I talked him into coming up here. If he'd have stayed in Denver he'd still be alive." Her torn habit had been carefully sewn, but still she kept a hand clutched over her chest as if she were afraid it might fall open at any time. She shook her head briskly. "It was my idea to pool our resources to buy land and build a joint church."

"It was a very good idea," Cord said.

But she didn't seem to hear Cord. "Why did I leave him all alone this morning? Alone so that evil man Dutch could sneak in and make good his threat. What kind of monster stabs an unconscious man to death?"

"The worst kind."

"If only someone had seen him do it, maybe we could have prevented it. But no, we were all outside witnessing bloody barbarism."

They walked up the main street, rutted and gouged from a harsh winter and heavy spring rain. Sister Agnes stepped on a hard dirt ridge and stumbled forward, grabbing Cord as she fell. He swooped an arm behind her back and caught her. "Whoa there. Watch your step."

She smiled politely. "Yes, thank you. It was nice of you to get me out of that stuffy old saloon to go on this walk."

"Well, now that I'm working for them, I do have some privileges. Besides they're all somewhat anxious to be nice to me, hoping that will influence my decision on their behalf. At least that's the pattern it's always taken before."

"There doesn't seem to be an honorable bone in anyone's body in this town."

Cord laughed.

"Oh my goodness," Sister Agnes frowned, clasping her hand to her mouth. "I didn't mean you of course, Mr. Diamondback. You've been marvelous."

"Thank you, Sister. You are a sister, aren't you? Or do you prefer to be called a nun?"

She smiled. "It doesn't matter. They're the same thing. Out here labels don't seem very important anyway."

Cord nodded. "Yes, you've certainly got your work cut out for you."

They walked on in silence, further up the mountain. The sun had slowly arced into the sky and was riding comfortably over a herd of woolly clouds.

Cord pointed to the side of the road. "Isn't this where you wanted to build your church?"

"Yes," she sighed sadly. "See how it would sit above the town like a monument. Like something worthy to achieve, a spiritual goal, if you will."

"Yes, it would be magnificent." He sat down on a large boulder, inviting her to join him. She did, wringing her hands and wiping the tears from her eyes as they sat. Cord reached over and cupped her hands between his own huge palms, rubbing them, calming them. He turned them over and examined the thick scars on her wrists. "Nasty looking."

She pulled her hands away and tugged her sleeves down. "I was young and quite foolish, with no spiritual sense. I'd lived a, well, soiled life once. A life of despair."

"We all have many lives before we find the right one," Cord said.

She forced a smile. "You're so kind, Mr. Diamondback. You seem to understand so much."

"I just don't want Reverend Kincaid's death to throw you off your goal."

"Oh, don't worry. No more knives across my wrists. Suicide is a sin, I know that now. Besides, I feel better knowing the man who killed the Reverend is also dead. God's punishment at your hands."

"Well, I usually work alone," Cord smiled.

Sister Agnes laughed. "Thank you so much for this walk. It's done me a world of good."

They ambled slowly back down the hill. Occasionally Cord would whistle a few notes of a popular song.

Sister Agnes stopped and studied his face. "I don't mean to pry into your methods, Mr. Diamondback. But since you promised those outlaws to have solved their problem by morning, shouldn't you be working on it now? I don't mean to sound unappreciative, but one day isn't very much time."

"Don't worry, Sister. I'm working on it right now. You'll see."

They walked a few minutes more, past the empty and boarded up stores that once bristled with eager miners anxious to spend their sudden wealth. Now they looked hollow and sagging and smelled stale even from a distance.

They rounded a corner past an empty dry goods store and found Victor "Angel Eyes" Curry waiting for them. He was half-sitting half-leaning on a hitching rail, his eyes hooded and brooding.

"Well, well, Mr. Curry," Cord said, his smile thin as a razor. "What a surprise meeting you here, so far from the center of town."

Curry pointed a finger in Cord's face. "Don't feed me none of your fancy bullshit, Diamondback. I went along with them others in hiring you 'cause it seemed right, not 'cause I like you."

"You went along with the others because you had no choice."

Curry sneered, but didn't argue. "Get rid of the nun, I want to talk business."

"Then your business will have to wait until I've walked Sister Agnes back to Fancy Dan's."

Curry thought that over a moment, his fingernails raking smooth skin as if checking for whiskers. "Okay, okay. It don't matter what she hears anyway. I'm offering you a deal."

"Where's your cousin Ray? Shouldn't he be in on this?"

"Ray's off sulking somewhere. He didn't take it too well when he found out about my old man and brother. He kinda liked them. 'Sides, it don't matter what he thinks anyway, I make the decisions for both of us. And Jodi too," he added with a smug grin.

"What's the deal?"

"Tomorrow you decide that the money should be split my way, and besides your fee, I'll give you a fair cut of what we get."

"How much?"

Sister Agnes gasped. "Mr. Diamondback, surely you wouldn't—"

"How much?" Diamondback repeated, cutting her off.

Curry twisted his cruel lips into a smile. "Five hundred."

"A thousand."

"Seven fifty."

Cord grabbed Sister Agnes' elbow and guided her down the street.

"Well?" Curry called. "How about it?"

"I'll let you know."

"When?"

"Tomorrow. When I announce my verdict."

Though she seemed somewhat confused by what had happened, Sister Agnes didn't question Cord as he returned her to Fancy Dan's Saloon. By now most of the men who knew how had been taken to the mines to work the claims another day, adding what meager gold they could find to the loot Diamondback was trying to divide. All that was left of the townspeople were the women and children, the elderly and sick, and some mechants who knew even less about mining than the amateurs out there now.

Cord knocked on the saloon door and ushered Sister Agnes in after a guard opened it. Cord nodded at the guard, who he recognized as Felix Clark, the young Englishman who'd come West looking for adventure. He wore his gun low on his hip, too low, Cord noted. And he'd perfected the contemptuous sneer they all seemed to have.

"I'll just be a minute," Cord explained with a friendly smile. "Want to pick up a few of my things."

Felix hesitated, then nodded. "All right, mate."

Cord led Sister Agnes through the crowd, though

it was far smaller than last night. When he found Gretel Peters, he smiled. "Hi, Gretel."

"Hi yourself, Diamondback."

Sven Regvall loomed nearby, his face still red and blustery.

"Sister Agnes here's been through a lot," Cord said. "I'd appreciate it if you'd keep an eye on her."

"Really, Mr. Diamondback," Sister Agnes said, "I am perfectly capable—"

"Now, now, Sister," Gretel winked. "Don't argue with him. It's best if we women just let the men think they're protecting us. Keeps 'em happy and out of our hair."

Sister Agnes smiled.

For a moment Gretel's face sagged. "It was Dutch that killed Reverend Kincaid, wasn't it?"

"Looks that way. After all, he did promise to fix him for interfering last night."

"Then what you did to that bastard wasn't mean enough. He deserved worse."

Cord nodded.

Sven Regvall had been pacing anxiously around the fringes of the group, now he couldn't help himself any longer. He marched over to Cord and, darting anxious glances at the watching guards, whispered, "What are you going to do about us?"

"About you?"

"*Ja*, us! We're in danger. The same thing that happened to that preacher could happen to us. Maybe they intend to slaughter us one by one. You've got to help us."

"Shut up, Sven," Gretel said.

"I will not shut up. I have a right to speak. It is this man's duty to help us. He is a judge."

"I'm a private judge. I only have to help my clients."

"But we need you," he cried desperately, spit spraying from his quivering lips. "It isn't fair, it isn't just."

Cord reached out and shoved the big man into a chair. "I don't want to hear about what's right or fair or just from you. In an ideal world maybe those men would all be locked up, or better yet they wouldn't even exist. But this isn't an ideal world, so we make the best of it we can." He leaned over the Swede, grabbing the big man's shirt in his fist. "This is a world in which justice is forged by *people*. The kind of people who think it's so important they're willing to risk everything for it. Justice isn't owed, it has to be earned."

Sven Regvall sat motionless, his eyes wide and frightened. Cord released his shirt, turned and tipped his hat at Gretel and Sister Agnes. "Good day, ladies."

"You're a hard son of a bitch, Diamondback," Gretel chuckled. "And that's just what this town needs."

"I've already got clients," Cord said and left.

"How much?" Cord asked.

Tom Delancy sipped on his beer and shrugged. "Three hundred."

Cord laughed.

"Four hundred."

"Curry's offered me $750."

Delancy turned and leaned his back against the bar, sweeping the room with his open hand. "I've got a lot of mouths to feed. Besides, I can back up my offer with manpower and firepower. Curry'll crap in his pants if it comes to a fight."

"That's something to consider," Cord agreed, slid-

ing his empty mug down the bar before heading
toward the batwing doors.

"Well," Delancy demanded. "What about my offer?"

"I'll consider it."

"When will you let me know?"

"Tomorrow morning, along with everybody else."

"Welcome to our hotel, Mr. Diamondback," Ulysses Quinn grinned. "It isn't much, but we call it
home."

"So does the owner," Cord said.

Ulysses shrugged. "Finders keepers."

Jason Quinn had changed into a white cotton suit
and was carrying a cane. Somehow the natty attire
seemed ludicrous stretched over his huge frame. He
moved behind the clerk's desk. "Any particular room
you'd care for?"

"Where's yours?"

"We're sharing the one in the corner with a view of
all three street corners."

"I'll have the one at the opposite end of the
building."

"Not very sociable, Mr. Diamondback," Jason said,
handing him a key.

"Perhaps you'd like a drink?" Ulysses offered. "Relax
a moment and chat."

Cord stared at the two men. They were large men,
but moved smoothly. They dressed well and spoke
well, itself a rarity among outlaws. Cord remembered
their names from when he rode in Texas with the
cavalry. The Quinns were wanted all over the state
for train robbery, bank robbery, stage coach robbery. If it had money, the Quinns would rob it.

Ulysses Quinn stood smiling, his thick lips lost
among the red beard streaked with grey. His younger

brother also smiled, his thumbs hooked in the sleeves of the white vest. The perfect picture of two quiet businessmen, marred only by the low-slung holsters of the professional.

"Let's skip the drink and get to business," Cord said. "How much?"

Jason looked at his brother. Ulysses' smile broadened. "I see we're not the first."

Cord shook his head.

"Second?"

Cord shook his head.

"Well, perhaps last, but certainly not least. For your sake." Ulysses cleared his throat. "An awkward position. Ordinarily neither my brother nor myself would stoop to bribery, but we find ourselves having to compete in a market with unscrupulous men, therefore, what can we do?"

"Pay up, I guess."

Ulysses frowned. "Yes, I suppose so. It's not unlike the Trojan War, eh, Jason?"

"Yes."

"You see, Mr. Diamondback, the Trojan War was basically started by a beauty contest between three goddesses, Juno, Venus, and Minerva. The judge was a shepherd named Paris. Like you, he didn't much like the job, because no matter who he picked, the other two would be angry with him. And being goddesses, they had the power to make him suffer when they were mad."

"I guess I'm the judge in this story," Cord said flatly. "Does that make you and the others goddesses?"

"Merely as an illustration of a point," he said with some annoyance. "As it turned out, each tried to bribe poor Paris, offering him wealth and glory. But Venus offered him the most beautiful woman in the world: Helen of Troy. Naturally, he chose Venus as the winner and got Helen. Unfortunately, Helen was married and thus began the Trojan War."

"Is there a moral here?"

"Isn't there always?"

"Do you mean one shouldn't take bribes?"

"Not at all," he smiled. "Just take the right one."

Jason leaned across the clerk's desk. "One shouldn't let women influence one's decision."

Cord tilted his hat back on his head. "You both sure know a lot about that ancient stuff, don't you?"

"Our father was a great Latin and Greek scholar. Read to us from all the great poets and poems. *The Iliad*, *The Odyssey*. Ovid, Virgil, Homer."

"That's some background for a couple of thieves."

"Well, our father was a great scholar but a lousy rancher."

"The worst in Texas," Jason agreed.

"He went through three wives and four ranches before he drank himself to death a few years ago." Ulysses smiled grimly. "There's not much room in Texas for Latin and Greek scholars."

Cord turned and started up the stairs, the key to his room dangling from his hand.

"Mr. Diamondback," Ulysses called after him. "You do understand our story, don't you?"

Cord stopped and turned around. "I understand this: it was prophesied when he was born that Paris would destroy Troy, so it didn't really matter which goddess he chose. The other two would have made sure he was punished."

Ulysses looked surprised. "You're familiar with the story?"

He smiled and continued up the stairs. "Mythology interests me."

* * *

Cord found the room that matched the key number, unlocked the chipped wooden door, and pushed it open. It was a modest room with whitewashed walls, a dresser with a drawer missing, and a wash basin and pitcher, both cracked. The bed was rickety looking, but the person sitting on it didn't seem to mind.

"Hi," Jodi said weakly.

"Hi, yourself. How'd you get in here?"

She pointed with her chin. "The Quinn brothers gave me a key. They said it was your room."

Cord hefted his own key and smiled thinly. The Quinns were a couple of very sharp customers. When tomorrow morning came, he'd want to make sure he knew where they were before delivering his verdict. "They seem to like you quite a bit," he told Jodi.

"What do you mean?"

"They compared you with Helen of Troy."

She shrugged. "They're nice, but spooky."

"Where's Curry?"

She examined the back of her hands. "I don't know. I left him. I . . . I just couldn't stand the thought of what he did to his pa and brother. I still can't believe I loved him." She shuddered. "Ugh. He laughed when I told him how I felt. He told me he was wanted in a lot of states for worse things than what he'd done to his family. Then after he was done describing each bloody detail, he wanted to . . . make love."

Cord sat down on the lumpy mattress and patted her knee. "What happened."

"I just ran out and came over here. I know I don't have any right to come to you, especially since I'm the one who got you into this mess in the first place.

But I didn't know where else to go. He's too good at tracking for me to just ride out on my own. He'd drag me back by evening and it would be worse for me."

"First of all, get that notion out of your head that you tricked me into coming here. I knew what it would be like even if you didn't. And second, you can stay here as long as you like and ride out with me in the morning."

She stiffened. "You're riding out in the morning?"

"Yes."

"But what about your decision?"

"I'll give it."

"And you still think they'll let you go?"

"Yes."

She shook her head. "I don't know who's more naive here, me or you."

He laughed. "Don't worry, I've got it all figured out."

"Maybe. But no matter who's position you choose, two of the gangs are going to be mad at you. And these men do bad things when they get mad."

Cord stood up and headed for the door. "I'll get you a room."

"What's wrong with this one?"

"Nothing, except it's mine."

She lowered her head, then raised it quickly to look at him. The little candles flickered behind the pale blue again. "So?"

Cord locked the door and returned to the bed, hanging his gun on the bedpost. "I wanted to thank you for saving my life this morning. It took a lot of nerve to pull a gun on those men."

"Oh shut up and make love to me."

Their clothes came off in layers of activity. A

flurry of arms and legs and a shirt and blouse would flutter to the side of the bed. Another flurry, more clothes. When they were naked, they took time to look at each other's bodies.

"I've never seen anything like you," she whispered, her fingers tracing the ridges of muscle along his chest and stomach.

He leaned over and kissed her firmly, crushing her lips, probing her mouth with his tongue. While they kissed, he could feel her tiny fingers gently sliding down his ribs, across his stomach, searching. When she found his swollen penis she wrapped her fingers around it and squeezed hard. He felt that familiar tingling across his skin like a thousand birds running across his back.

He began kissing her neck and shoulders, working his way down until he encircled her breast with his mouth. She sighed sweetly, her eyes fluttering a bit as he sucked the hard nipple up into his mouth. He rolled it tenderly between his teeth, feeling it getting even harder and longer.

Jodi began to writhe a bit, her pubic mound rubbing against his thigh with increasing pressure. He moved his hand down, prying her legs open, and slipping a finger into her sopping flesh. The opening was fairly big for such a small woman, so he eased two more fingers in. Her pelvis thrust forward to swallow his fingers and he could hear her gulping air.

"Please don't wait," she pleaded. "Please."

Cord lifted her legs off the bed, hooking one under each arm and spreading them as far as they would go. He looked down at her moist red pubic hairs, glistening from her excitement. They seemed to flicker like a fire just starting to burn. He smiled at that image as he plunged his thick penis into her, feeling her muscles grabbing at him, pulling him deeper.

He moved against her in a slow rhythm, gradually increasing. He was in no hurry. Sweat beaded across her forehead causing little wet curls to stick there. Her head was thrown back as she sucked air and strained to keep her hips thrashing in time with his.

His movements brought her to the edge several times, but then he stopped, letting her wait. They'd both wanted this for a long time, and he wanted it to be worth the wait. Now he began a more deliberate, insistent rhythm, pumping his penis into her with long deep strokes. She moaned softly, somehow knowing this was going to be it. Her breathing became even more shallow as she grit her teeth and concentrated on moving her hips.

At one point they both opened their eyes and stared at each other as they moved. This excited both of them and they began to move even faster.

"Oh, *please*," she sobbed.

Cord arched his back as he pounded against her, rocking between her sweaty thighs with urgency. The sound of their sex was like gentle waves slapping the sides of a canoe. Growing faster as the current carried them towards the bubbling rapids. She felt the pressure too as her buttocks leaped from the bed trying to merge with his tense body. She screamed loudly and he felt his body automatically thrust forward, the fire where they were joined consuming them both in delicious hot spasms.

Their bodies were both so slickered with sweat he slid easily off her, but enfolded her close to him. They kissed again, long and leisurely. She started to speak, but he smothered her words with another kiss. He didn't want words now. Soon she discovered neither did she.

It was dark by the time they exhausted each other's bodies. The moon was bright nestled among a crowd of stars, pouring blue light through their window.

Cord leaned over to kiss Jodi awake. "Time to get up."

She blinked her eyes open. "Wha-what time is it?"

"Night time."

"Good, we can start all over again."

He brushed the covers aside and hopped out of bed. "If you think I can do all that again right now, I'm not quite the man you think I am."

"Oh yes you are," she smiled playfully. "And more."

Cord pulled on his clothes and boots with swift economic movements. Jodi watched him from the bed with a grin. "You do that pretty fast. Lots of practice I bet."

"Yeah, I've been dressing myself everyday for years now."

"That's not what I meant."

He smiled. "I know."

"Where are you going?"

"We."

"Huh?"

"*We* are going. I'm taking you over to Fancy Dan's Saloon."

She bolted up, the covers tumbling off her breasts. "That's where the townspeople are kept. The prisoners. I'm not going there."

"That's the safest place for you right now."

"I'll stay with you."

"You can't. I've got work to do tonight."

"What kind of work."

He ignored her question. "Hurry up, Jodi."

"She tucked the covers tightly around her. "I'm not going," she announced with a stubborn pout.

"I can force you," he said quietly. "But I won't. I just wanted you safe. It'll make it easier for me to do what I have to do knowing you're okay. By tomorrow morning this will all be over and you'll be free. Trust me."

She sighed deeply and stepped out of bed. In the pale moonlight her naked body seemed to glow. Cord felt himself becoming aroused again, but tried to force those thoughts out of his mind. For one thing he had work to do if he still wanted to be alive tomorrow morning. And for another, he was too damn sore.

She dressed quickly. They both strapped their guns on at the same time, facing each other across the bed. When they looked up at each other they laughed.

Cord locked the door behind him and walked Jodi through the hall and down the stairs, keeping her on his left side so his gun hand would be free. The lobby was unlit and the Quinns were nowhere to be seen.

Fancy Dan's Saloon was only across the street, but as Cord lead Jodi, someone stepped out of the shadows behind them.

"Diamondback!"

Cord turned slowly. Victor Curry was standing four feet behind him, his gun still in his holster, but his hand hovering near the handle. His bandanna was crooked, revealing the tab of skin that once was his ear. The dark seemed to help the sparse hairs over his lip seem more like a moustache.

"I don't want to wait till tomorrow," he said gruffly. "I want to know what you're gonna say right now."

"Tomorrow," Cord replied.

"No! Now." His gun hand twitched but didn't draw.

"Tomorrow."

"Goddamn it, Diamondback, I deserve to know."

"How do you figure?"

"Hell, I let you fuck my woman, didn't I?"

Jodi gasped. "I'm not your woman, Vic. Maybe I was once, but never again. And I decide what I do with my body, not you."

He grinned wolfishly. "Shit, it ain't that much of a body to decide over." He snickered to himself. "Am I right, Diamondback. She's got an ass skinnier than a starving cat, ain't she?"

It was two steps to Victor Curry, and Cord covered them before the Curry was able to clear his gun from the holster. Cord knocked his hand away, tossed the gun far into the dark, and looped a full-force punch into Curry's stomach, lifting him off his feet. The air whooshed out of Curry with a cough as he crumpled to the ground, hugging his stomach and gagging for air.

"Tomorrow," Cord said softly, leading Jodi away.

Cord knocked on the front door and waited while the door was unlocked and opened. Ray Curry stood in front of them with a Colt Peacemaker .45.

"Hi, Ray," Jodi nodded.

"Jodi." He stood aside while they entered. "What do you two want here."

Cord looked around the room. It was still half-empty. "They got you guarding all alone tonight, huh?"

Ray Curry looked confused. He knew that Diamondback was no friend of his or any of the other outlaws here, so he didn't know how to act towards him. But he was a friendly fellow, and since he was deciding on how to split up the money, it couldn't do any harm to be friendly. "Yup, I'm alone. They're letting the men who worked at the mines wash off before bringing 'em back. Get's a might ripe in here otherwise." He hooked a thumb over his shoulder. "Ain't no need for more than one guard for mostly women and children and a couple geezers. 'Sides, there ain't a man in this town with guts enough to try anything."

Cord slapped him jovially on the back. "Probably right."

Ray nodded at Jodi. "Whatchya doing here anyway?"

"Hiding out from Vic mostly. He and I are through, Ray."

Ray shrugged. "I figured. He's a pretty mean cuss all right, but he seemed to have calmed down some since he took up with you. But I guess his true nature was bound to come out sooner or later again. Nature of the beast, I guess. Don't mind telling you, since I found out about what he done to Uncle Karl and Cousin Tim, I ain't felt too good about him myself."

"Okay if I stay here tonight, Ray?" Jodi asked.

"Sure. But you'll have to give me your gun. Can't take no chances someone getting it away from you."

Jodi looked at Cord, he nodded slightly.

She slid the pistol out of its slot and handed it to

Ray. He shook his head and grinned. "Damn rig never stops tickling me." He shoved the extra gun in his belt.

"I'm going to get her settled first, okay?" Cord said.

Ray cocked his head suspiciously because he thought that made him look smarter. "Suit yourself," he shrugged, returning to his perch on the balcony.

Diamondback guided Jodi around and over bodies until they spotted Gretel Peters and Sister Agnes.

"Well, well, if it isn't that hard bastard Diamondback," Gretel smiled. "Though he don't look quite as hard as last time I saw him." She giggled lewdly and Jodi flushed. Sister Agnes looked away.

Cord stooped down and took the old lady's hands. "Good to see you too, Gretel." He looked over his shoulder up at Ray Curry who was staring hungrily at a painting of a nude woman that hung over the bar. "You have a vet in here somewhere?"

She pointed at an old man sleeping on the faro table. "That's Doc Lakely."

"What kind of doctor is he?"

"All kinds. He's a people doctor, a vet, a dentist, a barber, a phrenologist—"

"A what?" Sister Agnes asked.

Gretel laughed. "Claims he can read the bumps on your head and tell you all about yourself."

"Perfect," Cord said and hurried off.

Doctor Lakely had a bristly grey beard to match his bristly grey eyebrows. His lips fluttered as he puffed air out with a loud snore. He wore a rumpled wool suit with several cigar burns on the sleeves.

"Dr. Lakely," Cord said.

No response.

"Dr. Lakely," he repeated, nudging the doctor's arm.

The old man opened his eyes and sat up looking as alert as if he'd been awake the whole time. There was a mischievous twinkle in his eye that Cord had seen before in men his age, and hoped to have himself when he got to be that old. If he lived that long.

"There's a price on your head, young man," Dr. Lakely said solemnly.

"Oh?" Cord remained expressionless.

"That's right. Want me to tell you how much?"

"Go ahead."

"One dollar. One single dollar. That's how much it costs for me to apply the great medical art of phrenology to your particular head. One dollar and I can tell you more about yourself than your own mother."

Cord laughed and tossed him two dollars.

"Ah, you must have a very large head, son. Just bring it over here and I'll show you what I learned from Dr. Johann Spurzheim himself. I can see by the slope of your forehead that you're very calculating and alert. Now, if you'll—"

Cord held up his hand. "Right now I'm more interested in your expertise as a veterinarian."

"Well, why didn't you say so? What can I do for you?"

After his talk with Dr. Lakely and receiving directions to the doctor's office, Cord started back for Gretel, Jodi, and Sister Agnes. His plan was already in motion. All he had to do was keep it rolling.

He stepped over a sleeping girl clutching a rag doll and was stopped by a big beefy hand on his chest.

"What you going to do?" Sven Regvall asked. Fear

had driven him past his normal cowardice. His eyes were bloodshot and rimmed with red skin. He was blinking nervously as he spoke, his accent getting thicker and thicker. "I asked what you do. You best answer, by *Gott*."

Cord brushed the hand away, but kept his voice even. It wouldn't do to attract Ray Curry's attention right now. "What do you mean, Mr. Regvall."

"What I mean? *Ja*, I tell you what I mean. I mean, what you do to help us? You goddamn judge. You s'pposed to bring justice."

"I told you, I can't bring that. It's not a gift."

He pressed closer to Cord, his thick neck turning red with anger. His breath was sour. "You got help. No one else. They got gun; give me gun. Then, by *Gott*, I show you." He stabbed his jumbo finger against Cord's chest.

"I can't help you. You'll have to help yourselves."

"You better help. You give me your gun." He reached for Cord's gun. Cord clamped his hands around the Swede's thumbs and bent backwards until Sven Regvall dropped on his butt with a loud thud. When Cord released the thumbs, the Swede pressed them under his arms and moaned.

Cord stepped around him and continued weaving through the people.

"I see Sven got a little testy," Gretel said.

"Nothing serious."

"Well, don't be too hard on him, Diamondback. He's old and poor and that's a mighty powerful combination working against a person."

"I know." He squatted down on his heels in front of Gretel and held her withered brown hands in his. "I don't have much time so I want you listen carefully. This is the best chance you'll ever have of taking this town back for yourselves and you have to take it."

"What?" Jodi asked.

"How?" Gretel asked.

Sister Agnes sat up and leaned closer.

"You'll have to take care of Ray Curry there before they bring the men back and post more guards. Once you've taken him, you'll have two guns, his and Jodi's. After that, wait until the men are brought back, then try to get the drop on the guards with them. There should only be two. Try and do that without firing a shot if possible so you don't alert the others."

"How do we take Ray?" Jodi asked. "He's armed and we aren't."

While holding Gretel's hands, Cord worked the Remington Over-and-Under .41 out of his boot and into her hands. She closed her hands over the small derringer like a clam over a pearl. He'd managed to recover it from his saddlebags earlier that morning after he'd dropped Sister Agnes off.

"You've got two shots here. That's all the help I'm going to give you. All I ask is that once you've overcome all the guards, you stay here for half an hour. Then you can do what you want, though I advise you to head for the Owl Creek Saloon where you'll probably find Victor Curry. He was already half drunk when we saw earlier. And after what happened he'll probably soothe his ego with another bottle."

"What about the others?" Jodi asked.

"Leave them to me."

Cord studied each woman in turn. They each had the same expression, a pale wooden frown that showed their fear, mixed with a grim sparkle in the eye that indicated excitement.

"We shouldn't take another life," Sister Agnes said.

"After what them bastards done to Floyd and the others?" Gretel snapped. "Like hell."

"That's for you to decide," Cord said. "I've done what I can. The rest is up to you."

He stood quickly and walked away without a word. He didn't want to debate anything with them. He had his plan worked out without them, so if they decided to pass, everything should work out the same. But he wanted to give them a chance to take their town back. A chance to earn that justice they cried for. It was a town of people who felt cheated by fortune. Who thought they'd been treated unfairly by life. This was their chance to get some of their own back. To take control. Maybe they were too far gone, too convinced they were losers. But it was important that they tried, that they risked something. Especially after what Cord had discovered that afternoon. Whether or not he told them that secret depended on what they did in the next few minutes.

As he watched Ray Curry come down the stairs to let him out, he could hear the mumbles over his shoulder as the word was being spread. But was it the word of action or passivity?

"Made up your mind yet which way you're judging?" Ray asked as he unlocked the door.

Cord smiled. "Can't tell you until tomorrow morning. Ethics."

Ray nodded sagely as if he understood.

"Well, good night," Cord said and turned to go.

" 'Night," Ray answered.

Cord stopped short at the door and pointed at Ray's gun. "Isn't that an Eagle-Butt Peacemaker .45?"

Ray smiled happily. "Sure is. Engraved with a genuine mother-of-pearl handle."

Cord looked impressed. "Say, can I take a quick look. I haven't seen one of those in a long time."

Ray hesitated only briefly, before slapping his pistol out of the hand-tooled holster and handing it proudly to Cord.

Cord made appreciative noises as he fussed over the gun. "Beautifully engraved. And the handle," he let out a low whistle. "It has the emblem of Mexico and everything. Look at that. An eagle biting a snake. Terrific." He looked down the sights. "How's she shoot?"

"The best equalizer I've ever handled. Me and Vic done a hell of a lot of killing down in Texas and Oklahoma, and this baby's got me out of more tight spots than butter in a whorehouse." He chuckled. " 'Course, we never killed nobody's father or brother like Vic done. That just weren't right. Killing's one thing, but killing kin's a whole other matter."

Cord listened to him talk as he examined the Colt. If he was right, Ray Curry was enough of a gunman to only have five of the chambers loaded, allowing the one the trigger rode on to be empty. Most everyone knew of one or two cowboys who didn't keep that empty chamber, most of whom had permanent limps or scars on their legs where the gun accidentally shot them. He was right about Ray; the one chamber was empty. "Feels good to hold."

"Good? Hell, that ain't the half of it . . ." And he was off again recounting close calls during holdups.

As he spoke, Cord nodded encouragement as he silently worked the cylinder around until the empty chamber was directly to the left of the hammer. He handed the gun back with an envious frown.

"I sure am jealous," Cord said, walking out the door.

"Most folks are," Ray called after him smugly.

Cord didn't stop to see what would happen. Either Gretel and Jodi and the others would take the chance and go after Ray or they wouldn't. Watching wouldn't make any difference. If they did, the first shot Ray took would hit an empty chamber. That would confuse him long enough for them to squeeze off a shot. And the derringer was small enough that the sound probably wouldn't carry. Well, he'd given them the opportunity, the rest was up to them.

He marched off into the dark street, his hand brushing the butt of his .45 as he walked. Just for the hell of it he checked to make sure the hammer was riding the empty chamber. It was. He thought about it a moment and thumbed another cartridge in. It looked like the kind of night where he'd need that sixth bullet.

21.

Diamondback moved swiftly through the dark streets, clinging to walls, staying in the shadows. He looked up into the black sky freckled with stars and tried to gauge the time. The Big Dipper balanced above and slightly to the left of the North Star. That made it about 9:00 P.M. He had to move faster.

Gretel's brothel was bubbling with activity. The three tired girls forced nervous laughter to match the drunken gruffness of Delancy's men. Occasionally a bottle would break or a chair would be smashed or a woman would squeal from rough treatment, all of which provided cover for Cord as he made his appointed rounds.

The first stop was the Owl Creek Saloon to check on Victor Curry. The saloon was completely dark as Cord approached. He eased out his .45 and ducked under the batwing doors, scanning the dark room for even darker shadows. Nothing moved.

He brought his gun chest level as he crept toward the bar in a crouch. As his eyes accustomed themselves, the darkness seemed to dissolve around objects, and the black lump on top of the bar became more familiar. It was Victor Curry, stretched out and sleeping a deep drunken sleep. Cord could smell the stale sour odor of booze and vomit and decided not to walk any further. He could see clearly from where he stood Curry's open mouth drooling into a puddle on the bar, his fitful breathing. He tip-toed out.

Following Dr. Lakely's directions were a bit difficult, but he finally managed to locate the tiny office at the back of the barber shop, which the doctor also ran. On the wall was a large phrenology chart of a skull divided like a side of beef showing which parts corresponded to certain personality traits. Next to that was a cabinet with the medical supplies Cord was searching for. He slipped what he needed in his pockets and left.

The livery stable was the same one he'd passed last night on the way into town. The one Floyd had dangled from. The horses were easy to recognize. Delancy's men's horses were of varying qualities, all boarded in the far stalls. The Curry cousins and Jodi's horses were boarded on the opposite wall. In between were two beautiful roans, well groomed and well-fed, that could only belong to the Quinn brothers.

It took Cord less than ten minutes to do what he'd come for.

On the way back to the center of town, he'd seen Reno Hernandez and Felix Clark herding the tired townsmen back toward Fancy Dan's Saloon. He pressed himself into the shadows and waited until they were all inside. He listened carefully, but no shots followed, which either meant that they'd taken them quietly as he'd suggested, or they'd done nothing at all. Either way, he had to move fast.

He did not try to hide his presence back at the hotel, stomping up the stairs, humming as he approached the Quinn brother's room. Sneaking up on them would have been difficult, especially since they're trained to expect it. But walking boldly in could confuse them slightly. Enough to get the drop.

When he found the room, he rapped his knuckles briskly against the door. There was no answer, just the whisper of metal sliding along worn leather.

"It's Diamondback," he said, knocking again. "I want to talk."

The door was unlocked and pulled open by Jason, who stood elegantly posed in his maroon satin smoking jacket, a pipe in one hand a gun in the other. The robe was unfashionably belted by a heavy leather holster. Sitting in the chair facing the door was Ulysses Quinn, his gun following Cord into the room.

Cord frowned disapproval at their guns, but said nothing. If they were going to put them away they'd do it without any comment from him. And there wasn't anything he could do but stall until they did.

Ulysses Quinn was barefoot and barechested, sitting there wearing only his trousers. His gunbelt straddled one knee and a newspaper folded over the other. He smiled at Cord though his eyes remained wary. "This paper's more than a month old. But Jason and I have been reading it everyday since we picked it up. I think the first thing we're going to do with our share of the money is ride to a city that has a daily newspaper. What do you think, Jason?"

"As long as they have a proper haberdashery, that's all I ask." He closed the door behind Cord and stood with his gun pointed at Cord's stomach, waiting for a signal from his brother.

Ulysses studied Cord in silence for a moment, then slipped his gun back into his holster, which he kept balanced on his knee. Jason also dropped his pistol back in his holster, but puffed on his pipe with his left hand, keeping the right dangling casually near the gun's butt.

"What's on your mind, Mr. Diamondback?" Ulysses asked. "You've reached a judgment?"

"Well, yes, in a way."

"What do you mean?"

Cord slapped his holster and his .45 was suddenly in his hand, waving the brothers to drop their guns. "I mean that you may not like my judgment. Leave the guns and grab your boots."

"Where are we going?"

"Wherever I say, I guess."

Ulysses angrily pulled on his shirt and boots. He didn't bother making any threats, but they were there nevertheless. In his flashing eyes.

Cord ushered them quickly across the street toward Gretel's place. He nudged them each in the back with his gun and they walked reluctantly through the door. They paused a moment, their two massive bodies filling the doorway as they surveyed the room.

"Let's go," Cord said behind them, and they entered.

The sitting room was lushly decorated, complete with crystal chandeliers, tiffany lamps, expensive rugs, and crimson wallpaper. Most of the expensive furniture was now damaged, torn or splintered from the gang's activities.

As Cord and the Quinn brothers stepped into the room, everyone stopped whatever they were doing. Even those that had been drinking too much seemed to instantly sober up. The sight of Cord's drawn pistol drew their attention. They began to slowly inch apart from each other.

"Just everybody stay where you are," Cord said, grabbing a frilly pillow from the sofa and pressing it in front of his gun barrel.

Everyone froze. Except Grover Benson, who thought he was out of Cord's line of vision. His movement was so slow anyway as to be almost imperceptible.

Cord swung around and fired. The sound was no more than a loud cough and the pillow spit feathers for two feet. Grover Benson yelled as his thigh sprang a forty-five caliber leak, blood squirting down the leg of his pants. He dropped to the floor clutching his wounded thigh.

"Goddamn it, what'd you do that for?" he bellowed.

"I told you to stay," Cord said. He turned back to face the others. No one moved.

Tom Delancy was sitting alone in an overstuffed velvet wingback chair at the back of the room, a bottle in one hand and a smoking cigarette in the other. He spoke calmly. "What's on your mind, Diamondback?"

Cord smiled. "I've reached my verdict."

Delancy stiffened in his chair, his stagnant eyes stirring. He rubbed his stubbled chin thoughtfully. "I'm listening."

Cord shook his head. "Privately."

Delancy looked at the Quinns, then back at Cord. "How we gonna do that?"

"If your men will keep the brothers comfortable while you and I step outside, I think we can quickly wrap this case up. Of course, if they try anything stupid, I'll pump a couple bullets into your brain."

Delancy rubbed his chin again and looked at Grover Benson wrapping a bandanna around the gaping hole in his thigh. He dropped the bottle on the floor, stuck the cigarette in his mouth, stood up and walked toward Cord, talking over his shoulder to his men. "I'm going outside. Just do what he said. Keep the

Quinns here entertained, but don't try nothing. 'Cause if you do and he don't kill you, I will."

Cord followed Delancy outside, his gun poking sharply in the outlaw's back. Once they were standing on the porch, Cord holstered his gun. "Question."

"Yeah?"

"With all the men you've got, why didn't you just take the money and cut out?"

Delancy flicked the cigarette butt into the night. It arced, glowed red, then died like a comet. "I thought of it a hundred times. But them Quinns ain't that easy to cut out on. I don't know how you got the drop on 'em so easy, but none of us coulda got within ten feet of 'em without bullets flying. Even if we could get away, I'd sure hate to have the two of 'em on my trail. Then too if we made a play against the Quinns, the Currys would have to take their side just to protect their own interests. Four of my men used to ride with the Currys and that might be pushing them some to expect them to come down on Vic already. The boss of a gang's got a lot of considerations."

"Well, I'm going to lighten your load a bit, Delancy."

Delancy's eyes brightened. "What do you mean?"

"I mean, I've decided in your favor."

"Equal split for each man?"

"Better," Cord grinned. "You're gang gets it all. I get my $5,000 plus a $500 bonus for keeping the Quinns off your backs while you ride free."

"What about the Currys?"

"Vic is out cold and Ray's got guard duty tonight."

"So do two of my men."

Cord shrugged. "You can't tell them what you're doing without tipping Ray. Of course you could kill him, but he might take a few of you with him. And the shooting would wake up Vic. That could get messy."

"Yeah, it could."

"I suggest you just grab the loot and ride out. Once you're gone I'll sneak a message to your men and they can slip out and join you later. Unless you don't want to tell them anything and split more amongst yourselves."

Delancy scratched his chin again. He was trying to figure how much more money it would be for each if they left two men behind. "After all," he concluded, "I got more men than I can feed now anyway."

Cord offered his hand and they shook. "Deal. Just make sure I get my cut. I've already saddled your horses."

Delancy grinned, his soupy green eyes narrowing to slits. "You've thought of everything, Diamondback."

"That's what I get paid for."

"Yeah. I knew what I heard about you couldn't be true. I told Dutch that it couldn't be."

"What's that?"

"That you couldn't be bought. Word had it that when you were hired you couldn't be bought. I knew that couldn't be so. Everybody can be bought."

"If the price is right."

Delancy laughed and slapped Cord on the back. "Ain't that so?"

Two doors down from the Owl Creek Saloon was the abandoned bank where the outlaws kept all the money, gold, and goods they'd gathered. It was within easy gunsight of any of the four buildings where they were staying, so no one could sneak up on it and steal it from the others.

It took Delancy and his men less than fifteen minutes to load it all up in their saddlebags, less Cord's cut, and ride quietly out of town. To prevent any premature alarm, they took Gretel's girls with them, promising to drop them off a few miles from town. When the last horse rounded the bend near the livery stable, Cord lead the Quinns back to their hotel room.

Ulysses smoothed his red beard and sat down with a sigh. "I'm a little disappointed in you, Mr. Diamondback. I thought you were a man who could be trusted to keep his word."

"I am keeping my word."

"You call this double-cross keeping your word?" his deep voice demanded angrily. "I hate to think what you'd call cheating."

"I agreed to find a just solution to your problem of what to do with the money. I have."

"Sure," Jason said. "You gave it all to Delancy in exchange for a bribe."

The two brothers glowered menacingly at Cord.

Cord holstered his .45 and leaned against the door. "What can you tell me about Virgil 'Red' Cummings?"

"Who?" Ulysses asked.

"Look, there's no time for any of that now. Red Cummings followed Jodi from here with every intention of killing us. Somebody from here sent him and I figure it was you two."

"I don't know what you're talking about," Jason protested. "We didn't send anybody to do anything. We don't even know—"

"How'd you find out?" Ulysses interrupted quietly.

Cord shrugged. "Lots of little hints. He came from Texas, but didn't want me to know. You two come from Texas. He was nicknamed Red after his father.

Both of you have red hair, even though he didn't.
You told me your father had married several times
and was a Greek and Latin scholar. You're both
named after characters in Greek mythology, and Red's
real name was Virgil, after the Latin poet your father
read to you from. I figured him to be a half-brother."

Ulysses nodded.

"The only thing I can't figure out is why you
wanted Jodi and me killed?"

"We didn't," Jason said. "We didn't tell him to kill
anyone."

Ulysses continued. "Red wasn't much of a brother,
not even half as much. He'd been mean and greedy
since he was little, and no one could do anything
about it. Not that we were much of an example for
him to follow. But we took up robbing to help our
father keep his last ranch going. He'd lost so much
already, we just couldn't see him lose it all again.
That's not much of an excuse, but at least we didn't
kill anyone. Red took up robbing as an excuse for
killing. He used his mother's maiden name because
he didn't want to be confused with us. He wanted
his own reputation."

"Well, he was bounty hunting now. I found a
poster for Victor Curry on him."

The brothers exchanged looks.

"We were all bounty hunters," Ulysses explained.
"Jason and I had an offer from the governor back in
Texas. If we brought in a few important outlaws,
he'd pardon us. He figured it would be easier for us
to get closer to outlaws than any lawmen. And he's
got an election coming up after promising for years
how he was going to clean up the state." He laughed.
"Anyway, it was a good deal so we took it."

Jason nodded. "After we got him to include Red

on the deal. He didn't want to, but we convinced him."

"Why?" Cord asked.

"He's family," Ulysses shrugged. "We figured we owed him one more chance. So the three of us came up here trailing Curry, found him riding with Delancy, and Jason and I pretended to join up. If we could take in all of them, that would be more than enough for our pardon. We were stalling until we thought of a way to take them all. That's why we told Red to trail the woman and keep her from bringing anybody back. He was just supposed to delay you, not kill you."

Cord opened the door and started out, pausing in the doorway. "If you hurry, you might still catch up with Delancy's gang. They have a head start, but it won't be long before that little something I gave their horses starts taking effect. They should be on foot within the hour. Easy enough to round up then."

Ulysses frowned, tugging on his beard. "I don't understand. What about the gold and the money?"

"I don't care what you do with it. Just don't bring it back here. You can turn it in in Texas and they'll eventually send it back. That might even make up for not bringing Curry in."

"What happens to Curry?"

"That's not your problem. Your problem is getting out of town as fast as possible, before the townspeople escape and all hell breaks lose."

"How are they going to escape?" Jason asked.

Cord smiled and closed the door behind him. He heard them scrambling to finish dressing as he clattered down the hall. He was halfway down the stairs when he heard two shots followed by the harsh yelling of an angry mob.

* * *

The crowd had split into three waves of attack, one for each building where the gangs had stayed. Cord caught twenty or thirty men at the bottom of the stairs. One brandished a gun while the rest waved bottles, table legs, or just fists.

"They've already gone," Cord shouted. "Let's try the saloon."

The mob roared its approval and flooded back out the door with Cord at their backs.

Cord saw the group coming out of Gretel's yelling loudly in confusion and frustration because there were no outlaws there. But the group chanting its way out of the Owl Creek Saloon was jubilant as they marched the staggering Victor Curry into the middle of the street. Fingers clawed at him as he was pushed along, and spit from the crowd dripped from his face.

"Kill him!" someone screamed.

"Get a rope!" someone else suggested.

Cord found Jodi in the crowd, her gun dangling at her side. He put his arm around her and gave her a hug. "Looks like you did just fine. What about the guards?"

"Ray's dead, the other two are tied up and unconscious. Gretel shot Ray and we used his gun to overcome the other two."

"Nice work."

"Thanks to Gretel."

"Damn right," Gretel said, sliding up to them. "I told 'em all I knew how to use one of these." She waved the derringer in Cord's face. "Used to carry one in my corset when I was just starting out."

Someone pitched Curry forward and he stumbled to his knees at Cord's feet.

"Where's Ray?" Curry rasped desperately. "And

Delancy? And the Quinns? Where the hell is every-body?"

"Yeah?" the crowd wanted to know. After finally getting the nerve up to do something, they didn't want to be robbed of their fight.

"They're all gone. They decided to take the money and leave these four behind."

"No!" Curry cried. "They wouldn't dare."

"They dared," Cord told him.

"Well, hell," someone in the back yelled. "We still got three alive. Let's hang 'em now."

Those in the front row looked at Cord as if they expected him to protest. He held up his hands and stepped aside.

"Do what you want. It's none of my business. You earned the right to practice any kind of justice you want."

There was a quiet contempt in his voice that ev-eryone picked up on.

"*Ja*, we must be careful," Sven Regvall said, step-ping up next to Cord and addressing the crowd. "We must be careful not to make ourselves bad like those men. We should wait for judge, hold trial. Do what is right."

"We have a judge," some one shouted angrily. "And we can hold our own trial."

Sven Regvall shook his head. His eyes were no longer red and frightened. The old man stood tall and spoke firmly. "No, Mr. Diamondback is good man, but not a judge for this kind of trial."

"He's right," Cord agreed. "This isn't the kind of thing I do. You need a legal judge."

There were some heated discussions, but no one made any moves. Finally the talk of lynching faded away.

"Thank God," Sister Agnes said, crossing herself.

Cord looked at her with a thin grin, revealing just a hint of teeth. "You're going to keep this up right to the end, aren't you?"

"Cord!" Jodi said, surprised by the harshness in his voice.

"What do you mean, Mr. Diamondback?" Sister Agnes asked, startled.

"I mean that you're a damn fine actress, but you're not a sister or a nun."

Mumbled bewilderment breezed through the crowd. Everyone strained closer to hear.

"Are you crazy, man?" the big Swede asked.

Cord reached out and grabbed one of Sister Agnes's wrists, yanking it palm up for everyone to see. "Take a look at these scars."

"Reverend Kincaid told us all about them, Cord," Jodi said.

"No, he only told you what she told him. Look more closely. See the pattern here along this thick one and how it curves up at each end? That's a rope scar, not a knife scar." He pushed her sleeve up to the elbow. "These are the scars of a gambler caught cheating. Because she was a woman they only hung her by her wrists for a day. If she'd have been a man they'd have hung her by her neck."

Sister Agnes pulled her hand away. "What makes you such an expert on scars?" she hissed.

Cord smiled. "You have to be out here. This land leaves its mark on everybody in different ways just to let them know who's boss. It's like branding cattle. Only we're the cattle. The missing fingers of the miner, the lame foot of the horse breaker, the bullet scars of the soldier. They tell you as much about a person as the clothes they wear. Sometimes more, because they can't be changed." He smiled at her. "And you really should learn more about the characters you're playing. To most people a nun and a sister are the same thing, but not to a devout Catholic. Their vows are different. As a sister, you should have known that when I asked you this morning."

"But why?" Jodi asked, facing the woman. "Why pretend?"

The woman pulled her veil off the top of her head and shook her full black hair into place. Her lips curled into a sneer.

There was something about the transformation of the sweet dutiful Sister Agnes into the grinning preening woman before them that sent a gasp through the crowd.

"You're doing all the talking, handsome," she said to Cord. "Why don't you tell them?"

Cord looked around at the crowd of townspeople, their faces weary from the ordeal, yet glowing from the fight, from the sense that they accomplished something together.

"I guess you earned the right to know," he said. " 'Sister Agnes' here tricked Reverend Kincaid into taking her along up here for one reason only. To buy land and stake claims."

Someone laughed bitterly. "Hell, I'll sell her mine. Ain't no need for dressin' up." A murmur of agreement rippled through the crowd.

"You may not agree when I'm finished. She didn't have money of her own, not much anyway. But combined with what Reverend Kincaid had to build his church, she should be able to get more land, and use that to buy even more. How she found out about it, I don't know. Probably from an amateur miner from here who pulled out and left a while ago. He probably didn't even know himself."

"Damn it, Diamondback," Gretel said. "Found out about what?"

Cord paused. "Silver."

"What?"

The crowd pressed closer, shouting out questions. Cord waved them quiet. "Silver's always been a problem to recognize, even for experienced miners let alone you folks. And since all the experienced prospectors left this place long ago, they weren't around when you slowly worked your way to the silver."

Someone in the back laughed. "What silver, man? there ain't no silver around here. Anybody see any silver anywhere?" He laughed loudly and was soon joined by others.

Cord smiled. "Like I said, one of the reasons so many abandoned mines have been reopened in recent years is that the first time through they only cared about gold. Then after the gold ran out someone would go back and discover silver. But the problem is in identifying it. It's looks different depending on where you look. At the Comstoke Lode the silver combined with gold and looked blue. In other places it can be yellow, white, pale green, dark red, or brown, depending on what other ores are in the ground."

"And what color is it here?" the man laughed again. "Pink?"

"Black."

There was a deep silence.

"There is a mighty lot of black ore further up the hill," Gretel said. "Most people figured it was some kind of carbon or something."

"It's silver. The good 'sister' and I took a walk up

there this morning to examine locations for the church she wanted to build. That's why she wanted her church up on the hill. She wanted the land. Unfortunately, Reverend Kincaid didn't see things her way and she killed him."

"*Gott*," Sven Regvall gasped. "Not possible."

"Isn't it? Ask her?"

She stretched her lips in a thin evil smile.

"My God," Jodi said and took an involuntary step backward. But it was one step too many.

Victor Curry lunged at the gun dangling at her side, snatching it out of her hand. Quickly he spun toward Cord, his eyes screaming.

Cord caught the first sudden movement out of the corner of his eye and started diving forward, shouldering Jodi and Gretel to the ground as he twisted to draw his gun. But he knew even as he fell that he would be too late.

"No," Sven Regvall shouted and shoved his huge body toward Curry, swiping at the gun with his meaty hands. The first shot caught him in the chest and spun him around with a shocked expression riding his face all the way to the ground.

The second shot came from Cord's .45. So did the third and forth. The first punched through Curry's throat, pumping a thin stream of blood out. His hands flew up to grasp the wound. But before they made it, the second and third bullets spun through his jaw and cheek, sending scraps of torn flesh and shattered teeth into the crowd as his head whipped around in a spray of bloody pulp.

22.

Dr. Lakely stood back and admired his work.

"How am I, Doc?" Sven Regvall asked from the bed.

"You're lucky. Swedes have higher foreheads than most. Shows an ability to endure pain and recover quickly. Unfortunately, their temples show that they're slow to pay bills."

"Nay, Doc, I pay this one soon as I get up."

Cord offered his hand. "Thanks for saving my life, Mr. Regvall."

"I think maybe I should thank you for saving mine," he replied quietly shaking hands.

"Get some rest, Sven," Dr. Lakely advised. "Gretel insists on making you some of her homemade potato soup, and you'll need your strength to recover from it. She makes the worst potato soup in the world."

Cord and Dr. Lakely walked down the stairs and joined the others in the hotel lobby. Most of the townspeople had gone home to straighten out their families and be together. A few had made a makeshift jail out of a storage shed and tossed 'Sister Agnes' and the two outlaws in it.

"He'll be fine," Dr. Lakely explained to Gretel and Jodi as he and Cord entered the room. "The bullet was deflected by a rib. He's lost some blood, but not enough to endanger him."

"That son of a bitch will feel a lot better after he gets some of my famous potato soup," Gretel said, still waving Cord's derringer as if daring someone to disagree.

Jodi sat quietly, pale and shaken. Her hair hung disheveled around her face as she nervously twisted the ends. She looked drained. Of blood, of energy, of feelings.

Cord sat on the sofa next to her.

Gretel looked the two of them over and elbowed Dr. Lakely in the side. "C'mon you old bastard. Let's go grab a buckboard and pick my girls up. Afterwards you can help me peel potatoes." She winked at Cord and dragged the doctor out the door before he could say a word.

He looped an arm around her shoulder. "What now, Jodi?"

She shrugged. "Go home, I guess. I just wasn't as smart as I thought. I was a fool about Vic and I guess about everything else. Nobody is what they seem out here."

"Are things clearer in Kansas?"

"I don't know. But the one time I'm out on my own I botch everything up. I almost got you killed and the whole damn town destroyed to boot. Maybe I'll go back to Washington."

He laughed. "Talk about nobody being what they seem."

She turned her head and looked at him, her eyes brimming with tears. Then she coughed out a laugh, and another, until they were laughing together.

"There's room here in Dog Trail," he said. "Within a year there will be ten thousand people living here, maybe more. You could be anything you wanted here. Start your own business, mine a claim. Whatever you want."

"Yes," she said brightening. "Yes, that's right. I could." She pressed his hand next to her cheek, kissing his knuckles. "What about you? What are you going to do?"

"Ride over to Denver and wire San Francisco to see if there are any more jobs for me. If not I'll live off the fee I made here for awhile until a judging job comes along or a fight."

"How about staying here?" There was expectancy in her voice but no real hope.

"Sure, for a few days. I believe my room is paid up."

"You mean our room," she laughed. She reached over and slid her hand around his neck, pulling him close for a long moist kiss. "Besides, I intend to use this time to convince you to stay longer."

"Start convincing," he grinned.

She stood up and grabbed his hand, leading him up the stairs to the room. She was already unfastening her blouse as they went through the door. With a shrug and a grind she stepped out of her pants and flung off her blouse. She stood in front of him naked, swaying in a teasing manner.

Cord was out of his clothes and standing in front of her.

"Just one question," she said. "How come you know so much about nuns and their vows and such?"

Cord smiled. "Nuns interest me."

And he reached out and swept her onto the bed, already locked in a kiss as they fell.